I0553251

THE FALL LINE

Other Books Written As Ute Carbone

Dancing In The White Room

Written As Annie Hoff

Georgette Alden Starts Over
The P-Town Queen
Afterglow

Deslisle Publications

The Fall Line
Wild Snow, II

By

Ute Carbone

CLIMAX, SK
CANADA

Copyright 2020 by Ute Carbone
April 2020
ISBN 978-1-989276-17-4
Cover Art by JE Smith
Produced in Canada

Dedication

For Jim.

Acknowledgements

There are a group of writers who have given me support and encouragement through all my writing trials and tribulations and to whom I owe more than I can ever repay. Carolyn Saari, Kate Johnson, Tammy McCracken, Sherry Steffensmeier, Suzanne Ahmad, Fran LeMoine, Tresa Jones, Deborah Jelley, Alex Hayes, Kathy Pyle, Harriet Reindeau, Suzanne Schryrver, and Lana Ayers—thanks for listening and writing and sharing.

And special thanks to my editor, Diane Badzinsky and to Ellen Smith, for giving a home to my books.

Prologue

Mia

My last big win is burned like the brightest of memories into my mind. I can still hear the music, the hard beat of the grunge I listened to before each race, blasting thought my earbuds as I went over the course in my head. I can still remember the course, one of a million sets of slalom gates I've run in my life. If asked, I could still pantomime the movements through those turns, though each gate, as I had on that day.

I can see coach Marv signaling me, am still jolted by the sudden silence as I shut off the music and stuff the buds in my gear bag, I can hear the snap as my boot meets and joins the binding, feel the snow under my skis as I skate over to the start house, my limbs willing and anxious, the short wait already too long. There were cowbells ringing, they'd announced Tin's finish time and I remember thinking not bad, probably enough to push her into third place and being happy for my best friend and best rival. I remember Tin's crackly voice on the walkie talkie as I waited for Elena Marks, the Canadian star, to finish her run.

"Let it all out at the end, Ice. You got this," Tin said.

"You got this. Just smooth out, don't miss and you got this," Coach repeated.

I took my place in the start gate and clicked my poles together three times for luck. My name was announced over the speaker and the count began—ten, nine—at zero, the start bar bumped my shin and I was off. The world a blur of white, nothing but snow and ice and speed, my skis an extension of my body, my breathing in tandem with each turn.

One turn and the next and the next, I let out fast and hard, the sun on my back, the gates coming at me as I chase them down and devour them. By mid-course, I knew I could win. By the last gate, I knew I would win. There's a final skate, a push across the finish, my heart racing now as I turned to stop and pulled off my helmet in one continuous motion. My name flashed on top of the leader board. I was ahead by half a second.

Tin rushed toward me, nearly bowling me over. "Hot damn, girl!" She hugged me and I felt tears sting my eyes.

They announced Katya Hofstadter, the only woman who could still have beaten me out for the world cup, though she'd have needed a phenomenal run to do it. "I can't watch," I said, only half kidding as I buried my head in Tin's shoulder.

I looked up as her mid-course time flashed on the board. Two hundredths of a second slower than me, it was going to be close. Katya skied into the finish, and the five seconds it took for her time to post on the leader board seemed like several eternities. Her name popped up under mine. Three hundredths of a second slower than me. And just like that, it was done. I had won my sixth world cup

Everyone gathered around me, hugging me, congratulating me. I was so high with winning I flew outside of my body, light as air, turning somersaults in the brilliant blue winter sky overhead.

If I had known what the next year would bring, I would have hung on to the feeling; I would have kept hanging on to it for all I was worth.

Part One
Before

One

Mia

The summer before it all changed, my life was so busy I barely had time to sleep or brush my teeth. Between training with the team, there were TV appearances, interviews, and even a visit to the White House. It was August by the time I had a chance to catch my breath and visit my home town. My boyfriend, Connor, picked me up at the airport in Manchester, New Hampshire.

"So you're a legend now," he said as we cruised over the highway toward home.

"Yeah. I plan on making it seven titles," I said raising my brows.

"You're not getting any younger."

"Thanks a lot, baby. I love you, too."

Coming into my hometown, there was a newly painted sign that read "Franconia, New Hampshire, home of ski champion Mia Whitmeyer." Connor grimaced at it as if it had somehow done him wrong. I should have asked, but I didn't. After kissing me with half-hearted enthusiasm when I'd come off the plane, he'd been quiet for most of the long ride home. It bothered me, and had I been less travel weary, I might have confronted him about it.

At the inn my parents owned another large sign said, "Welcome home, Mia!"

"My dad had the Sports Illustrated cover framed. He's my biggest fan, it's almost embarrassing," I said. I'd been the cover story a few months back and my Dad had been more excited than I was. I think he told everyone in town.

"Did you mean what you said in the article?" Connor asked.

"What did I say?" The reporter and I had talked about skiing and racing, things sports fans would be interested in.

"About retirement not being on the radar."

"It's not. Just because I'm the oldest woman on the team does not mean I'm over the hill. Why, do you think I'm old?" I smirked at him, though I was irritated. It was the second time he'd brought up my age.

"No, of course not."

The day after my homecoming, Connor and I hiked to Lake of the Clouds. I had grown up in the White Mountains and this trail, lacing its way through the presidential range, was a favorite of mine. We got up to the ridge and sat on the rocks, overlooking the stony peaks and green hills all around us. The wind whistled through the pines, and the sun poked in and out of puffy clouds. It was a warm day, balmy by mountain standards, and so I took off my pack and put my head back, closed my eyes, and let the breeze cool my arms as the sun caressed my face.

Connor had again been exceptionally quiet on the hike up and, again, I had the feeling that something wasn't quite right. I tried to tease him out of his mood. "Maybe some nude sunbathing is in order," I said. "There's no one here." I put my hand to his thigh as he sat next to me.

He pulled back as though I'd scorched him with a match. "I can't do this anymore."

His words caught me way off guard. "What's wrong?" I asked.

"I'm...it's been, what, ten years? How long are you going to keep racing?"

This was the third time he'd brought up my age and my irritation with his constant question was beginning to turn to anger. I tried to look him in the eye, but the bright light put him into relief, and the only thing I could make out was a dark outline of his face. "The Olympics are less than two years away. I have to be there. If you know me at all, you know that."

"There's the trouble. I do know you. You said after the last Olympics you'd consider we get married."

"I do consider it. It's just..."

"It's always 'just something'. If it isn't the Olympics, it's the World Cup. I've never been first on your list. I'm not even sure I make your list."

"I don't have a list, Connor. I don't have some hidden agenda."

He'd gotten up from the rock and was looking out at the sea of green trees below us. A few years earlier, he'd asked me to marry him and I hadn't said no. I'd said later. Maybe, though, there was a limit to his patience. Maybe I hadn't been fair to him. I got up and stood next to him and put my arms around his waist. "Do you want to get married? I travel a lot. I'm hardly ever here. But if you want to do it, you know I will. In a heartbeat."

I didn't get how bad things were until he turned to look at me. There was something in his eyes I hadn't seen before. "I've met someone. You don't know her; someone I work with. It's new and I don't know where it's going yet."

You know what they say about not appreciating what you've got until it slips through your fingers? Connor might as well have punched me in the gut. I crossed my arms as though I could protect myself from further hurt. "You've met someone? As in friend? As in dating? Or are you sleeping with her? What?"

The lines of Connor's mouth tightened. "We've gone out a few times. Nothing more. I want to be upfront. I wanted to tell you before things got any more serious."

"That's damn nice of you."

"I'm trying to do the right thing here, Mia."

I grabbed my pack and began to walk and then run back down the trail. I didn't let myself cry until I was halfway down the mountain. I was a hot mess by the time I got to the trailhead parking lot. There stood Connor's new SUV, a Honda Pilot big enough for a busload of people. That morning I'd joked about him wanting to field his own baseball team, meaning he'd want kids someday. I'd always thought I'd be part of the team, but now? Maybe it was someone else's team he was getting ready to field.

The thought made my stomach clench and then some resolve kicked in. I took out the mini pack of tissues I had in my pocket, blew my nose and wiped my eyes. For good measure, I got my water bottle, tipped back my head and poured the water on my face. I dried my cheeks with my forearm.

The trailhead was about five miles down the road from my parents' house. Since the last thing I wanted was to share car space with Connor, I decided to walk. As I hiked along the shoulder of the highway, my hurt evolved into anger. How dare Connor find someone new? He was supposed to love me. He was supposed to be there for me.

I'd been on the circuit for ten years and I was on the road most of the time. Long distance relationship didn't begin to describe what Connor and I had, we spent far more time apart then we did together. Yet, in all that time, I had never once cheated on him. There had been plenty of opportunity. And once, I almost gave into temptation, I almost left him for someone else. I hadn't let myself. I hadn't given in. I'd been loyal to Connor even when I hadn't wanted to be. I thought that counted for something, but I had been wrong.

A few miles into my walk, Connor's SUV came up behind me and pulled over to the shoulder. Connor jumped out with the engine still running. "Mia, stop."

I kept walking. He came up behind me and took my arm. "Why do you have to be so damn stubborn?"

I swung around. "Why do you have to be a lying asshole?" I stared at him. My eyes are blue and once upon a time, a reporter had referred to my pre-race concentration as 'an ice-ray stare'. The stare would have worked to convey my anger if my eyes hadn't started filling up again.

"I guess I deserved that." The tears softened Connor's voice. I hated that they worked this way. "Will you at least let me drive you home?"

I should have said no, I should have kept walking, but I climbed into the SUV. Maybe there was still some part of me that hoped he would apologize and say it was all a big misunderstanding. That of course he still loved me.

"I can stay for the party if you want," he said. My parents were planning a get together for about fifty friends and relatives.

"I don't want you to stay," I said as he pulled into the driveway. "I want you to leave. Right now. Leave and don't come back." It was a tad dramatic, I'll admit. I wasn't by nature a dramatic person, but mixing anger and heartache can do that.

"Mia, please. This doesn't have to be so hard. I still haven't made any decisions. I still care about you."

His words just served to fuel my temper. "Oh, so now I'm still in the running for the Connor O'Keefe prize? Here's the thing, I don't want to be. I'm withdrawing from the competition." I got out of the car. "Have a nice life."

I guess I'd made myself clear. He didn't try to follow me into the house. Half of me wished he would bound up the front porch steps, get down on his knees and beg my forgiveness. When I heard the car pull out of the drive behind me, I knew that wasn't going to happen. And I knew it was over

My folks didn't say outright they were having a party in my honor, but they wouldn't be having one if I hadn't been visiting.

The last thing I wanted was to be clapped on the back by people I'd known since I was in a highchair. But my folks had sacrificed a lot for my racing career, even taken out a second mortgage on the inn to cover travel when I was still a junior racer. They used to get up at the crack of dawn to take me to training at Cannon when I was a kid. They'd come to all the Olympics I'd competed in and every time I raced in the east, I could count on them being in the stands to cheer me on, no matter how awful the weather. They deserved a big share of the credit for what I'd been able to accomplish and if they wanted to have a party, the least I could do was paste on a smile and make the best of it.

Everyone kept telling me what a star I was. I didn't feel much like a star, I felt second rate, the girl who couldn't keep her man. "You put Franconia on the map," said Sam Helmstead, an old friend of the family. "You must need an entire museum for all those trophies."

My Aunt Patty, standing next to me, said "She keeps them here, isn't that right? Alex has an entire bookcase dedicated to them in his office."

My dad did have a display case of trophies and medals in his office. I was proud of them, sure, but he was prouder, and I liked that I could give him those tokens for all he'd done over the years.

"Would you like to see them?" Dad, standing nearby, had overheard our conversation. He beamed at me and handed me the key to the office. "You do the honors. You earned them."

"Which is your favorite?" Nina Helmstead asked.

I shrugged. "If I had to pick, it would be the gold from the downhill in Turin, I guess. It was my first Olympic gold medal."

Dad reached in and retrieved the medal from the case and hung it around my neck. "Pretty, isn't it?"

"Would you like to try it on?" I asked Nina, because having everyone stare at me was a little unnerving.

"You mean it?"

I took the medal from my neck and hung it around Nina's. Her husband snapped a picture of us.

"I'd love one of you and Connor," said Aunt Patty. "I haven't seen him around, where is he?"

I took a deep breath. How could I have imagined no one would notice Connor's absence? "He couldn't make it. Work." I caught my father's eyes as his look went from proud to concerned. "He's up for a VP job; it's a lot of responsibility right now." This much was true, and maybe Dad would buy it.

"Well." Aunt Patty took my arm. "Good on him for being ambitious. But if I see him, I'm going to tell him he ought to pay some good attention to his pretty girlfriend if he doesn't want her stolen away by some other young fellow."

She hadn't done it on purpose, but it felt like she'd taken a rusty knife and stabbed me with it. The room felt too small and crowded. "I'm going to go get something to drink," I said.

"There's my girl," Mom came over to me as I got a cola from the bar. "Where were you? And where is Connor?"

"Dad and I were giving the trophy tour. And Connor couldn't make it."

"Couldn't make it? Why? He was here this morning."

"I don't want to talk about right now, okay?"

"Okay." Mom looked me over. I figured my injuries had been tucked away under my stuck-on smile, but I was pretty sure she could see them. "Listen, sweetheart. If you want to go on home, you go ahead. Everybody's had the chance to talk with you. I'll just tell them you had a headache and you're tired."

Her kindness brought tears again. I didn't really want to just slink off, it felt wrong. But I was more afraid of breaking down into a messy heap in the middle of my parents' party. "Thanks, Mom. I'm sorry."

She kissed my cheek. "You've got nothing to be sorry for."

The house where my parents lived and I had grown up in was next door to the inn. I let myself in, music and laughter coming from next door with the party still going strong. I went to my bedroom and collapsed on the bed. I couldn't stay here, couldn't face any more questions. I was contracted to do a commercial spot in Chile at the end of August. The team trained there for a few weeks off season, and the Chilean government was promoting tourism, particularly some of the great skiing around Valle Nevado. Being a champion skier sometimes served up these opportunities, and while I wasn't exactly rich, they paid well and allowed me to make a decent living.

I went to the computer and re-booked my flight for the following night.

My mom knocked on the door as I was packing. "What are you doing?"

I eyed the half-packed suitcase, the shirts and jeans and jackets spread over the bed and felt as though I'd been caught committing a crime. "I'm leaving for Chile tomorrow."

"That isn't for another two weeks, is it?"

"No. I just need...I don't have much time to ski for fun anymore. I thought I might treat myself. The tickets are paid for and—"

My mother put her hand on my arm before I could finish. "Mia, what is going on with you?"

I thought I could still bluff my way through. Telling the truth would reduce me to another puddle of tears. "Nothing."

I might have known she wouldn't buy it. "You haven't been yourself since Connor dropped you off this morning. And then he's a no show at a party. Is there something going on between you two?"

I swallowed again and sat down next to the suitcase. "He...we broke up."

"Oh honey, it's probably just a little spat. You and Connor have been together a long time, you'll figure it out."

"He's seeing someone else." The words were hard to bring up. In them was every defeat I'd ever suffered.

"Oh." The news even left my mother speechless.

"So, you see, I can't stay here right now. I have to go. I can't..."

"You go to Chile. That's for the short term. But what about in the long run? You're going to have to deal with this."

"What I'm going to do is win myself a seventh cup. I'm going to do that, and nothing else is going to matter in the meantime."

My mother did not look convinced, but she said, "Okay, Mia. You do what you need to do." Then she sat down and put her arm around me. "But you're a champion no matter what happens. Win or lose, you're special to me and your father and a whole lot of other people. I want you to remember this. Promise me."

"I promise," I told her, although I felt anything but special.

Connor texted me the next morning, "We should talk." I didn't answer him. Last thing I wanted was to talk over what had happened between us. I turned off my phone.

Two

The ski season was going full tilt in Valle Nevado. I checked into the hotel, telling myself I'd enjoy room service and hit the slopes. I'd ski all day just for fun. I didn't get to ski for fun much anymore and refueling my passion for the sport seemed a good idea. The team coach, Marv Eagan, was always telling us how we needed passion.

I loved Coach Marv. He was tough as shoe leather and he could be a bear during training. Some of the girls complained about how hard he pushed us, but Marv had been my coach since I'd been a dewy-eyed newbie and I doubt I would have had the career I'd had so far without Marv pushing hard from the sidelines. I liked his toughness and I knew he admired the same trait in me.

I spent the first day in Chile sleeping. It had been a long plane ride, and all I wanted was a soft bed. By day two, I was out on the slopes. I skied all day and then did a few hours in the gym, wanting to push myself hard enough to leave no time out for brooding. It worked and that night I slept deep and long. On day three, it rained and I got out my rain gear and had the slopes to myself. I came in at dusk wet and hungry. My thoughts managed to catch up to me, as much as I tried to out ski them, and I felt sad and alone and sorry for myself.

Christina Renton, known to everyone as Tinny, was my best friend. We'd come through a lot together and I loved Tinny, at least I loved her when she wasn't trying to knock me off the board in a race, which she was more than capable of doing. And, honestly, if anyone other than me had to win, I would want it to be Tinny every time.

The ski season and training went on for about ten months out of the year, so Tin and I spent a lot of time together. In the hiatus, we messaged back and forth and usually called each other every day or two. Besides Coach, I often felt Tinny was the only one who understood me, and understood the dedication it took to be a world class racer.

"Where the hell are you?" she asked when I finally managed to call her.

"I'm in Valle Nevado. Hey, you should come on down. We could have fun and party for a week, get out all the bugs before we have to go back to training. What say you?"

There was silence on the other end of the line. "Tin?" I asked, wondering if I'd lost the connection.

"Jesus, Mia. I've been trying to reach you for three days. What the hell?"

"I have no phone service. You know how it is with overseas. No biggie. I had to pay for Wi-Fi to get onto a network, so I kinda put it off."

"Coach had a heart attack."

"What? Is he okay?" I thought maybe there was a fissure in the line. Coach was in his late sixties, but he was fit as a teenager. He could out-fit me on most days, and I prided myself on my muscle-to-fat ratio. "Where is he? Back in Boulder? I'll catch the next plane out of here."

There was silence again on the line, then a deep intake of breath that knocked my own breath away. "He's gone, Mia."

"What do you mean, gone?" I stared at the mirror next to the bathroom; it reflected the jumble of clothes coming out of dresser drawers, my stuff scattered everywhere. I should straighten up. If I did, Marv wouldn't be gone.

"The funeral's day after tomorrow in Boulder. Me and the other girls—you should be here, Mia. He would want you to be here."

Numb, I hung up and made a reservation for the next flight. I don't remember getting into Denver, just the airport, busy and noisy and me getting lost trying to find the right bus to the car rental place.

"How long do you need the car for?" asked the cheerful blonde behind the Avis desk.

"I don't know."

She stared at me, "You need to tell us how long you want to rent the car for."

"I don't know. A week, a month, what the hell does it matter?" Get a grip, I told myself. "A week," I said, mostly because I didn't want her to call security.

Tinny had grown up in Boulder, which was also Marv's hometown, and a few years back, she'd bought a house, a little bungalow on the outskirts of town. She lovingly decorated the place and called it her retirement home.

It was a cute little house, with a big porch hugging the front with flower boxes of geraniums. Tinny had, in typical Tin fashion, painted the place turquoise, which sounded like a crazy choice, but it looked good and gave the house an individual kind of flair. She answered the door, wearing her usual sweats and T-shirt, her feet bare. My hands started to shake and I gripped tighter onto the handle of my suitcase. "Hey, Ice," she said, using my nickname.

"Hey yourself." A few tears came out as we squeezed each other, though not enough to unfreeze the block my body had become.

"I made pizza. And I have Stoli."

"Can we skip right ahead to the Stoli?" I asked.

We went to the kitchen and she poured us each a glass. "The funeral's at nine," she said.

"I bought a black dress in some boutique yesterday. I hope it fits." I had a hard time with clothes, as I was six foot even in stocking feet.

"It'll be fine. Hey, it's good you came." We ate

Tin's homemade pizza in silence, each of us picking at the food. Tin's boyfriend, Jack, texted that he'd come to the funeral. "He's been like a rock through this," Tin said. "I don't know what I'd do without him. "

"He's a good guy," I agreed.

"Speaking of guys," Tinny refilled my glass with soda and a splash of vodka. "Is Connor coming out?"

I took a deep swallow, my head spinning and not because of the vodka. "Connor and I split."

"Oh, shit. Mia, I'm sorry."

"Yeah, it's been a hell of a month."

Tinny put her hand on mine. "One day at a time, isn't that what they say at AA?"

"Things keep up, I might need sponsorship." I took a swallow.

Coach Marv's funeral was packed with people from the ski racing world. The air conditioning in the church was on the fritz and it was about ninety degrees that day. Tinny and I and four other girls were in the A division, and we were referred to and called ourselves the A team. We were, or had been, Coach's girls. The six of us sat together in a pew, me between Tin and Lara Brandt, a quiet girl who had newly moved up from B. I hadn't been to many funerals and I didn't know what to expect. Mike Granberg, the head of U.S.. ski racing, said some things about Marv's stellar career. We sang a few hymns and then the pastor said we were all invited to a reception at a local banquet place.

The banquet hall was out in a wooded area. With a huge park-like garden and a gazebo, it looked more like a place to hold a wedding than a funeral. There was a buffet, with food piled high, though none of it seemed very appealing. After giving Marv's wife, Nell, a hug and saying how sorry I was, I sat down with the girls from the team.

"I hear Davey's getting Marv's job," said Irene, called Reni, Auckland. Davey was one of the assistant coaches. A few coaches had retired in the off season, and there was talk of some moving around, even before Marv had died. It churned my stomach to think on it now.

"Man, Davey. He's such a hard ass," lamented Rachel King. Rachel and Davey had a long history of run- ins, last year he'd nearly kicked her off the team for staying up and drinking half the night. She somehow managed to pull down great times despite her partying and so he had no justification for doing it. "Whoa, who's that?" Rachel pointed a plastic fork in the direction of a man talking to Nell Eagan.

Dark hair, tall athletic physique, Creech Crèches was the kind of handsome you don't soon forget. I hadn't forgotten him, though I hadn't seen him in eight years and the last place I would have expected to run into him was at Coach's funeral.

"That's Creech Crèches; he was my coach in the development levels. You think he's the new assistant?" asked Reni

"Ooh, man, he can assist me any time," said Rachel.

"Jesus, Rachel, it's a funeral," I hadn't meant to go at her, Rachel was just being Rachel, but if I was unnerved before, I was ready to come entirely unglued now. "I'm going to get some air." And with that, I left my half-eaten plate of food and headed for the door.

I went to the gazebo, sat on a bench and put my head between my knees. The roses growing up the trellis gave off a cloying smell and bees buzzed around, threatening to sting. Creech Crèches, what were the odds?

"Hey."

I pulled my head out from between my palms to see him standing at the edge of the gazebo. He had a little indent in his cheek when he smiled and hazel eyes that reminded me of the woods at home. Would the sight of him smiling still make my heart flip? It had been eight years. We were at a funeral. But the answer was clearly yes.

He wasn't smiling now. "I wanted to say hello before I took off. I'm really sorry we had to meet like this."

"Why are we meeting like this?"

He stopped to consider me for a minute. "I'm taking over for Marv."

"You are? You?"

"Is it that surprising? I just found out this morning."

Connor had busted my heart, and I'd lost Coach Marv. I started to laugh at what fate had brought and then the tears came. Me, Mia Whitmeyer, the girl who was nicknamed Ice, was sobbing uncontrollably in a hot gazebo surrounded by roses and bees. All of it witnessed by Creech Crèches. "I'm sorry," I managed.

"You're allowed emotion once in a while." He sat down next to me and bad went to worse as I sobbed into his shoulder. His hand was stroking my hair and it felt like it belonged there, but it didn't. I pulled away.

"I better get back inside. The girls will wonder what happened to me," I said, staring at the wet spot I'd left on the lapel of his jacket. And then I got up and went back in, without turning around, because I might have turned into a pillar of salt if I had.

Three

Creech

When I'd met Mia, years ago, I was brasher, full of bravado, maybe crazier, too. I was fast and I was going to be on top of the world racing order. It wasn't an idle brag on my part—I had spent my first year on the team on the C squad, and raced so well that I was put on A my second year. It meant I was one of the top six racers in the country.

In those days, we didn't have the huge training facility they have now, and Mia was just starting out, so her poster wasn't one of the first things you'd see when you walked into the lobby. But we had a facility and there was a lounge, a place to relax and take it easy or recover from a workout. It had a smoothie fountain and a café with all sorts of good-for-you foods at one end, and an ancient foosball table at the other.

We played foosball in between training sessions and we were, as always, cut throat competitive. The day I met Mia, I was playing against Pete Russ, a guy from B team who had been my roommate. I was heavy into it and annoyed when Pete suddenly stopped playing. "Who is that long, fine, drink o' water?" Pete was known for his hyperbole when it came to women. He was a great athlete, competitive to a fault, but very shy around girls so his proclamations always made me grin.

I looked up to see what he was on about. The girl walked in like she owned the place, tall with a blonde braid that hung down her back and nearly touched her waist. Right away she churned my insides with an instant attraction, though it was a fairly common reaction for me when seeing a pretty woman, so I took

the tightening in my gut in stride. "I'm going to find out."
I left Pete standing at the table, and even though I knew
he'd never be bold enough to walk up to her and
introduce himself, I wanted to be first.

She was getting a strawberry yogurt, so I grabbed
one for myself, tore out my near empty wallet and said,
"It's on me."

Her eyes met mine, eyes so blue they nearly
stopped my heart. She smirked at me. "Are you always
such a big spender?"

"So, I'm Creech. And you would be?"

"Creech, that's an interesting name."

"It's a nickname. My name is Joel, but don't call
me that. You might have heard of me, I'm on A team."
Makes me cringe to think I actually thought the A team
thing would impress her. "You still haven't told me your
name."

"No," she said, lifting up the yogurt in a toast. "I
haven't. Thanks for the snack, Joel." And she walked
away. I wanted to run after her like a puppy, but I had
enough pride not to do it. She'd gotten to me, though,
and now I wanted her. I wanted her big time.

Mia

"Rumor has it the guy at the funeral, Creech
Crèches, is the new coach," Tin said as she drove us
back to her house. "He was coach in development, he
must have been pretty good for them to bring him in."

Tin had come up a few years after me, by then
Creech had left the circuit. "He used to race. He was on
A team back when I started."

"Yeah, I vaguely remember the name being
battered around. Then he just left?"

"He took a really bad fall in a training run. He
never made it back after that, I guess. Went into
coaching instead."

Tinny pulled the car to the shoulder. "Oh, shit." I
couldn't for the life of me figure out what was wrong. My
mind was on Creech, his fingers in my hair. He'd been

so damned sweet this afternoon, and now he was filling up my head space.

Tin got out of the car, the engine idling, and ran to the gully by the side of the road. She put her hands to her knees and threw up all the funeral food she'd eaten. I got a tissue from my purse and handed it to her. "You okay? What happened?"

"I don't know." She took the tissue and wiped her mouth. "It came on me all of a sudden. It's probably stress, this has been one hell of a week."

We got back in the car. Grief affected people in different ways, true enough. I worried over Tinny anyway. We'd been in stressful situations before and some girls actually did throw up before big races. Tin had never been one of them.

She insisted she felt better and I was too wrung out to argue with her. As it was, we both took a nap when we got back to her place. I lay down on her guest bed with the curtains shut and closed my eyes, I tried not to dwell on the funeral, and Coach, which felt so raw it hurt every time my thoughts touched down there, or Connor, the other sore spot in my head space. I thought instead of Creech, those gold flecks in his hazel eyes, looking at me with such tenderness, and tears rose again, unbidden.

My parents' inn and restaurant in the White Mountains was a family operation, with my mom acting as manager and my dad, a chef, in charge of the kitchen. Some of my fondest childhood memories are of watching my dad cook. He taught me some of the basics and I found it very relaxing to mess around in the kitchen. I offered to make paella for dinner and Tin was only too happy to let me do it. It kept me occupied, going to the store for the ingredients and then putting it together with Tin's limited kitchen accessories, which was a challenge.

Jack, who had gone back to work after the

services, joined us and the three of us sat with a feast-load of food. The problem was none of us felt much like feasting.

"This is great," Jack said. "You could open a restaurant if the whole ski thing doesn't work out for you."

"Yeah, it's good to have a fallback position," I said.

"Since the ski thing's worked out pretty well, I don't guess you'd need a fall back." He smiled at me and then turned to Tin, gazing at her in a way that made me feel like a third wheel. He hadn't been in her life for long, they'd met the year before. She was a goner from the start and I couldn't much blame her. From where I sat, he was perfect for her—quick to laugh, easy going, and, more importantly, an avid skier. And he was clearly smitten with her. Judging by the shaving stuff and the extra toothbrush in the bathroom, he was spending most of his time at Tin's.

When Jack stayed the night and I crawled into the guest bed, alone, I missed Connor badly. I wanted someone in my life, someone I could lean on when things got rough, as they had now. But, if I was totally honest, I'd never had with Connor what Jack and Tin seemed to have. Maybe Connor had been right; if I had a list, he wouldn't have been at the top of it. I didn't much like the way this reflected on me.

I stayed with Tin for a few days and then went back to Chile to do the shoot, although the last thing I wanted to do was smile for the cameras. Luckily, filming only took one day, though it was a very long day and I was exhausted at the end of it. After I was done, I was at a loss. My parents were good at respecting my space, but they both wanted me to come home for a while and I was determined not to run home to lick my wounds. Besides, the last thing I needed was to run to into Connor or, worse, Connor and the new girl. I needed time and distance.

My legal address was in Park City, Utah, which was where we trained. I'd bought a condo a few years ago, a small one bedroom with a stone fireplace and a three-season porch shaded by aspens and overlooked by the mountains. It was all mine though I was gone too much to ever consider it, or anywhere, home.

I told my folks I'd see them in the winter, we were scheduled to ski at Waterville Valley in December, and I caught the next flight to Salt Lake City and headed into the mountains. When I got to my condo, I sank down into the leather couch and wrapped myself in the Navaho blanket I'd bought in Taos. It felt good to be in my own space.

I figured I might as well use my time well so the next day I went to the training center. The place was new and state of the art, with any kind of equipment you could imagine. I did a full workout in the weight room and then figured I'd treat myself to a yogurt smoothie in the nutrition center. The nutrition center was empty when I walked in, except for one table. And there sat Creech with his laptop, sipping a smoothie that was a ghastly shade of swamp green.

I don't know why I should have been so surprised to see him there. He was a team coach, my team coach. We were going to be spending a lot of time together, which meant I had to get over this infatuation, or whatever it was, and fast, if we had any chance of working together.

Best to go head on into the breach, I figured. At least I wasn't currently reduced to a puddle of tears. I got my drink and sat down across from him. "Fancy meeting you here."

He closed his computer and cleared his throat. "Yeah, how about that? What are the odds?"

"What are you up to?" I nodded to the laptop and hoped fervently he wasn't scoping porn sites.

"Looking for a place to live, actually. There are thirty zillion condos and none are in my price range, which is ten to twenty dollars a month for rent. What brings you in early?" He smiled and the little dimple in his cheek didn't do anything to quell the infatuation factor.

"I love this facility and I need all the help I can get. I'm not as young as I used to be." God, if I kept on like this, Creech would be tempted to search out a nursing home for me.

"Judging by the massive poster of you in the visitor's lobby, I'd say you don't have anything to worry about."

"You're only as good as your last race, Coach."

There was an awkward silence. I had known Creech long enough to know he wasn't the silent type. I nodded to the laptop again. "I live over in Aspen Heights. The units are nice, not too pricey. There might be something available," I said, going from nursing home resident to real estate agent in a single sentence.

"Thanks. I'll check it out. We could be neighbors. I'll come borrow sugar."

I pointed to his drink. "I don't think sugar would do anything to help that mess."

"Kale smoothie. It tastes surprisingly good."

"It looks surprisingly awful."

Since neither one of us had anything more to say about his shake, the conversation thudded to another halt. This was going to be so much harder than I thought and to make matters worse, my palms were beginning to sweat.

What the hell was the matter with me? I hadn't won six World Cup championships by being unhinged. I was known for cool, clear-headedness. Here I was letting an ancient short term relationship get under my skin. I took a deep breath. Go for it. "This is awkward."

"No kidding."

"Maybe we should clear the air. What happened between us is in the past, the way past. I'm willing to put it behind me. You do your job and I'll do mine."

He cocked his head, another habit that I'd

forgotten about and it made me want him more. "I wasn't about to relive the past, Mia. It's not my style. You are an amazing racer. I want to keep you in the standings. Nothing more."

"Good. Then we're both on the same page."

"Great."

"So, if you want to check out the condos, let me know."

"Thanks, I'll do that."

I walked away, the air clear. So why did I feel so disappointed?

Creech

I want to work with you, nothing more. I was such a liar. A good one, too, because I was pretty sure she bought it. Truth was, the whole time we were talking, all I could see was the full red of her lips and the way her hair kept falling out of the ponytail she'd tied it into. I wanted to push the strands of hair back and feel those lips against mine.

After my botched attempt at hitting on her, all those years ago, I had the chance to watch her ski in training camp. She came up on B team but she wouldn't stay there for long. Any fool could see that just watching her—she was like a panther, attacking the gates and gobbling them down. I realized telling her I was on A team was like telling Eric Clapton I could play guitar. If I wanted to impress her, I was going to have to find another way to do it. Maybe honesty would work; I went up to her at the recreation center and told her I was an idiot.

She grinned at me. "Yes, you are."

"You are impressive. I'd like to start again. I'm Creech and I'm not worthy."

That made her laugh and I bought her a Coke and after that she and I talked and joked a lot, though she was also quick to tell me she had a boyfriend. I sensed she was warning me off and I respected the boundary.

The men's and women's teams each have their own stops on the circuit and it isn't until the finals that both teams are in the same place at the same time. So Mia and I went our separate ways and didn't meet up again until the end of the racing season. The finals were in Val d'Isere, in the French Alps, that year. Like most of the places on the circuit, Val d'Isere was a resort town and you couldn't walk two steps down the main drag without passing a bar or a club. We racers weren't supposed to go out on the town, but we were young and had too much energy and long as we didn't get into any real trouble, or let it affect our racing, the coaches looked the other way.

Val d'Isere was the first big win for Mia, she took a gold in the super G, a combination of downhill and slalom that would become her best event over the years. The night after her race, a bunch of us went to a club, an international bunch of somewhat crazy racers who were high on skiing and life in general. The place we went to had a huge dance floor and a live band that sounded pretty good, and I asked Mia to dance. She could move. I think every male in the place had his eyes plastered on her as we danced, wild and fast and free. Then the song ended and a slow song started, I opened my arms and she walked into them, and there we were, the muscles of her back against my palms, her head in the hollow of my shoulder, her breath on my neck. When the music stopped, she looked at me wide eyed, her lips open as though to say something, but she didn't say anything, she went back to the table, got her jacket and said her goodbyes, saying that she had a GS in two days. Joking Coach still had a curfew and he'd kill her if she broke it.

"I'll walk you back," I offered.

"No. Stay. I'll be fine," she said. And then she was gone.

A lot of time had passed since then. She had

become the best women's racer in the world, well on her way to becoming legend. I admired and respected her for it. I was a good coach, good enough that the US Ski Association had entrusted me with their elite racers. I would keep her in the standings and I would keep my personal life and my feelings out of bounds. And yet, I could still hear the music and feel her in my arms. When the music had stopped, I'd wished the song had never ended.

Four

Mia

I went back to my condo, an analysis of my conversation with Creech like monkeys chattering in my head. I put on my runners and jogged to the trail through the brush and aspens behind my condo. It was varied terrain, up and down hill, and the weather was autumn crisp even though it was still August. I had to concentrate on my footing, to keep from tripping over roots and stones and this kept my thoughts from wandering around and made them stay with my feet and my pulse and my stride.

The trail was just over four miles long and I was nearly done, my mind gone comfortably blank, when I managed to trip over a rock and take a nose dive into the bracken alongside the path. Exasperated at my stupidity, I got up and took a few tentative steps. No pain, no weird feeling, which meant I'd done no real damage, though my arms and hands were scraped by the underbrush. I walked back to the condo feeling as though the trail had spanked me. I'd take a long, hot shower, which should set me back to rights.

I opened the door of my apartment to find Tinny sitting on the couch. She had a key, so there was no question of how she got in, it was more a question of why. She had made some small utterances about coming up early and hanging out, though it didn't make sense, since Jack was a bigger draw and should have kept her in Boulder until training started officially.

Her eyes went right to my scraped arms. It must have looked worse than it was. "I had a fight with some bracken. The bracken won," I said, coming over to give her a hug.

I expected her to come back with some snide remark about my lack of balance or the might of bracken or something, but she didn't say anything, just clasped me tight and held on as though I were a lifesaver in a raging sea.

"You're early," I said when she finally let go and sat down again. "I didn't think I'd see you for another week at least."

"Yeah, I know." Tin reached into her jacket pocket and pulled out a plastic stick in a zip lock bag and handed it to me. She bit her lip as I examined it.

"Pregnancy test?" Then I noticed the big plus sign on the end of it. "You're pregnant?"

Tin put her head into her hands in answer. "We were really careful. I don't get how it happened."

"What does Jack say?"

"He wants to get married. Soon as possible." Tinny started to cry, which was alarming because Tinny was not a crier.

"What are you going to do?"

"I don't know. I told Jack I had to come up here to settle things. But I don't know." She wiped her cheek with the back of her hand. "I was ready to have the best season of my life. I was rising in the standings last year, I figured I could make the podium a few more times. I was going to give it my all, and give you a run for your money." She sniffed and smiled. "The timing for this is so fucked up. But if I terminate the pregnancy, Jack wouldn't forgive me. It would be the end of us and that's the last thing I want."

I sat down and squeezed her hand. "How do you feel about having a kid?"

"I want kids. Jeez, I want kids with Jack. Just, I wasn't thinking this year, you know?"

"You could come back, still make it to Sochi. Look at Valeria." Valeria DePerna, an Italian skier, had not one but two children. After each pregnancy she'd come back and she was a force to be reckoned with, one hell of a competitor.

"I've never felt about anyone like I do about Jack. I can't lose him, Mia."

"Then I think you've already made up your mind. You're just getting used to the idea." I thought again of Creech, if the timing had been right, would I be with him now? Time had blurred the feelings I had then, and so it was hard to know if his coming back had brought those old emotions back into focus, or if these feelings, which I couldn't seem to out run, were brand new.

Once she'd made up her mind, or at least figured out what her heart had been telling her all along, Tinny went into resolve mode and was full of energy. We talked until two in the morning, mostly about her plans and Jack's and how she would handle all this change.

"I'll be back," she said in her best Terminator imitation. "Meantime, you have to beat up those damn Austrians all on your own." The Austrian team was a powerhouse and always had a new skier or two coming up to challenge us. All the competition kept us on our toes; even the competition, friendly though it was, between Tin and me made me ski harder and better. I didn't know what I'd do without her, and I told her so.

She waved it off. "You can handle it." Then she turned serious. "Besides, I'll still call to bug you. You're going to have to learn to knit; I'll need a bunch of booties for the kid. And you'll be godmother, we expect many gifts."

She would have to resign from the team, which meant she'd have to go see Creech. She was nervous about this. "I wish I knew him a little better. I met him at Coach's service for about two seconds. It'll be like going up to a stranger and saying 'oh by the way, I quit.'"

"Leave of absence. Not quit. I won't let you quit. You want me to come with?"

Tin considered. "You know him a little, right?

From a long time ago."

More than a little, I didn't say. "We were on the circuit together, my first few years, and his last."

"I could use the moral support, I guess." Tin shook her head. "I feel like I'm headed into uncharted territory with this whole thing. Wish I had a road map."

"No map. No GPS. You will be terrific though, I would want you for my mom."

That made her laugh. "Okay, kid, it's late and you are rubbing your eyes. Off to bed with you."

We slept late the next morning and then went to the training center. Creech had a small office, crammed with equipment, which seemed to cover every available surface and most of the floor space. There was a desk, where Creech sat with his laptop. He got up when we walked in, made his way around two pairs of stray skis and shook Tin's hand. Then he glanced at me and his smile faded. "What the hell happened to you?"

I examined my arms, I'd all but forgotten about the scrapes and scratches. They must have looked worse than I thought. "I had a run in with some underbrush while jogging yesterday."

He took my wrist in one hand and turned my arm elbow down, then took the fingers of his other hand and ran them over the deepest scratch. "You are using something to keep it from getting infected, right?"

His fingers made my whole body thrum and I worked to keep my voice even. "I put some antibiotic stuff on it. And I washed it with soap and water. It's fine."

He held my wrist a minute more, maybe a minute more than was necessary, then let go. "No more crawling through the briars, okay?"

"Yes, Coach." I looked to Tin; it was her we were here about.

Tin took a deep breath. "I have some good news and some bad news," she said. "The good news is that I'm about to marry the love of my life."

Creech raised his eyebrows. "And now I have to

ask you what the bad news is?"

Tin nodded. "I'm going to take a leave from the team. Seems the love of my life and I are having a baby."

He didn't answer her for a moment, I think she'd surprised him and he needed to gather his thoughts together. "Wow," he said finally. "Well, congratulations."

"She's coming back." I hoped to take the awkwardness away, but I could hear how I sounded as I said it, as though I were a kid insisting Santa was real. Although, honestly, I did believe she would come back. She was Tin and, like me, ski racing was a huge part of her life. Leaving it behind would leave a big hole, for her and for me. "I'll whip her back into shape myself, if I have to," I added.

Creech smiled at that, but there was something kind of wistful in his eyes, as though I'd reminded him of something else. I was probably just speculating, as I was feeling a bit wistful myself. "Sometimes, things change," he said. "Life changes and you move on. I'm really sorry I didn't get to know you better. You'll be missed around here, but I wish you every happiness."

Tin had a flight out that evening, so we stopped at the local deli for sandwiches and juice and took them down to the pool at the condo complex, where we'd hang out for the afternoon. "I'm going gluten free for a while after this," I mused aloud. I was in great shape, yet every year when training started it was an adjustment, and I began watching what I ate carefully.

"Ha." She took a bite of her tuna on rye. "I'm going to eat whatever I damn well please for the next nine months. Though I'll probably throw this sucker up later. Morning sickness my ass, more like all day all night sickness."

"You make it sound so wonderful."

She smirked at me. "You know, I think it will be. You should try it out yourself."

"You need a man for that sort of thing, I hear

tell." I took a bite of my roast beef with horse radish.

"I think Coach Crèches would be willing to help you out." I nearly choked, enough so that I had to take a swig of juice and Tin laughed. "I saw the way he was looking at you, the way he stroked your arm. If your scrapes had been any worse, he would have taken you on his desk."

My face got hot. "Well, that would be real appropriate, wouldn't it?"

"I'm not talking about propriety, Ice. He wants you. And I think maybe you want him."

"All right, I admit it. He's hot. Doesn't matter, anyway. He's the coach, so he's off limits." My next thought was that maybe, once upon a time, he wouldn't have been off limits. But back then, there'd been someone else and she wasn't me.

That first year, the year we met, we saw each other a lot while we were training in Park City. I did pretty well, and there were hints of my making A team once I had a few good races under my belt. We were to start the racing season in Switzerland, at Grindlewald. We spend a lot of time on the road, and most of it spent in the Alps in Europe. I think I've been to every European ski town by now, and most of the resorts in North America, too.

I was pretty nervous about traveling. It would be my first trip overseas and moreover, I was going without my folks, without Connor, without the kids I used to hang with. I'd just turned eighteen and wasn't much more than a kid myself. The night before we left, I found myself lying wide awake in my dorm room at midnight, staring into the dark, excited and a touch anxious. When I get that way, I've always found exercise helps to ease things; a good run would usually clear my head. It was late, too late to jog around in the woods, but the room was too close and sleep too elusive, so I decided maybe I should get up anyway. I got dressed in the dark, so as not to wake my roommate, and snuck out. If anyone asked I would have told them the truth, I just needed some fresh air. Outside the dorm was a small grassy area with several picnic tables and that's where I headed, thinking it was so late I'd have the place to myself. I could sit at the table, gaze up at the stars and get hold of my thoughts.

As it turned out, I didn't have the place to myself. Creech was sitting at one of the picnic benches, his back to me with his arms stretched out along the length of the table, his head tipped looking to be doing exactly what I had contemplated. He didn't see me at first, and I thought about sneaking back inside, but decided I wasn't ready to do that and besides, his being here shouldn't keep me from doing the same.

I took a few steps and he heard me, because he sat up and turned. "Hey, what are you doing here at this hour?"

I walked up to him until I stood in front of him. "I could ask you the same question."

"I couldn't sleep. I like sitting out here in the quiet sometimes."

I didn't know him that well, but from what I'd seen, I hadn't imagined he was the kind of guy who liked contemplating life in quiet solitude. It made me see him in a new light, and he looked very attractive in it. "Me neither. I mean I couldn't sleep, either."

He touched the place next to him on the bench. "I wouldn't mind company."

I sat down next to him, close but not touching, though I thought I could feel heat coming up from his arm. He tipped his head back again. "It's kind of soothing, to look at the stars."

"I wouldn't have taken you for a romantic."

He turned to examine me, a slight smile playing on his lips, the one I'd seen before, something I'd come to think of as 'Creech harmlessly flirting'. "Maybe you need to know me better." Then he leaned back again. "So, you want to talk about why you can't sleep. I'm a good listener. Not really, but I'll listen to you."

"I don't know. Nervous energy, I guess. I've never

been to Europe, and some of the women I'm racing against? I have posters of them in my bedroom. It's a little weird, you know?"

He laughed. "Someday, I'll bet some little girl will have a poster of you in her bedroom. You are destined for greatness."

"Uh huh, sure." I did, quite honestly, believe it even then, although I never would have admitted it. "It's just hard, so far away from the people you care about."

He didn't say anything for a minute, then said, "Yeah, that's the hardest part." And then, after another moment of silence passed, he added, "I'm here with a pretty girl, though, so I'm happy."

"No, you're not."

He sat up and stared at me, the flirt in his body language disappeared. "What makes you say that?"

"Just a hunch. You were sitting out here alone. That's a sign of something, right?"

"Maybe I'm nervous, too." He looked away again. "I got a call from my ex-girlfriend. She's at Middlebury College. She's dating someone new, she's moving in with him after graduation."

"And she called to tell you that? Ouch."

"Not ouch. Mallory and I have known each other since before we could both walk. She and I will always be friends, even if the romance kind of died an early death."

"You must still care about her; otherwise you wouldn't be out here."

He looked at me and smiled. "And then I would have missed the opportunity to sit here with you."

I ignored his trying to change the subject. "If it were my boyfriend doing that, I'd tell him to go fuck himself, just saying."

His smile faded and his jaw tightened. "You don't know me. You don't know her."

"You're right. It's just, well, I think you're a pretty nice guy from what I've seen and you deserve better."

He got up and brushed down his jacket. "Good

luck in Switzerland." And he walked away. I should have let it go, but I liked the way he'd opened up to me and I felt as though I'd let him down.

"Creech, wait. I'm sorry." He turned and stood with his arms crossed as I caught up to him. "I should think before opening my mouth. It's none of my business."

"No," he said, "it's not."

"Friends?"

He looked me over. "Sure, why not?" We walked back to the dorm in silence. The subject of his ex-girlfriend was never mentioned between us again.

I'd wondered about her though, and I wondered about her now as I took another bite of my sandwich. I remember wishing at the time that I had that kind of effect on Connor. The truth was and is I never had. And, if we're only given one chance, I'd blown mine and Creech had used his on some girl I'd never met. Maybe she was in his life, it was a long time ago, but maybe there was a happy ending for the two of them. Despite myself, I really didn't like the idea of him with someone else.

Five

A few weeks after Tin left, I saw Creech unpacking the back of an old pick up with New York State plates a few buildings down from my own in the condo complex. I was going for a run, and thought I might slip by unnoticed, but he looked up and so I jogged over.

"I owe you thanks," he said, hauling a large cardboard box from the back. "I found a condo I can afford the rent on here."

I watched his forearms cord as he lifted the box and knew distancing myself had done nothing to cool the thoughts in my head. "Just around the corner from me, looks like. I'm over in G, around the back."

"We'll have to compare, I wonder if the apartments are all alike. Though the back ones have a great view of the butte, whereas the one I rented has a great view of the parking lot and the road. But that's okay, it's nice and roomy." He nodded toward the truck bed. "These boxes have been back there since I packed up and came out here. My furniture's on its way, currently on a U-Haul truck with my two brothers, speeding across Nebraska."

"Is that your subtle way of asking for help with moving in?"

He grinned and my heart melted as though it was ice cream and he was hot fudge. "If you've got a few minutes, I wouldn't mind some help."

I grabbed a box, thinking maybe I should have told him I was busy after all, my hauling boxes for him was a bad idea, because it meant going into his apartment, which was exactly what my over-excited inner crush girl wanted.

His condo was nearly a replica of my own, except it had two small bedrooms to my one large one and I did have a better view. It, like mine, had a cathedral ceiling in the great room and, empty of furniture, the room looked deceptively large. Creech put the box he was carrying down near the fireplace. "It'll look better once I get the rest of my stuff. Though I might have to put some of it into storage."

I examined the ten boxes we'd hauled up the stairs. Furniture notwithstanding, it hardly filled one room, let alone four and a porch. "You had a mansion back in New York and you're downsizing?"

He laughed. "I am the proud owner of a dilapidated farmhouse. Four bedrooms, leaky roof and a bathroom with rusty pipes. It needs a lot of work. Still, I don't think I want to sell it. I managed to rent it out, which is how I'm funding this place."

"The farmhouse is in Lake Placid?"

"Wilmington, actually. Not far from Whiteface Mountain."

"Why wouldn't you want to sell? It's a long commute from here."

He ran his finger over the tape along the top of the box. "I don't know. I kind of love the place, I guess. It's nice to think a piece of my life is still back there, waiting for me to return to it." He shook his head. "Sorry, I'm getting real sentimental in my old age."

"No. It's nice you feel that way about a place." I thought of Tin and her house in Boulder, with Jack's toothbrush in her bathroom. And then I thought of how, when I went back to Franconia, I stayed in my childhood bedroom. Was there some lack in me that never considered buying a house, maybe with Connor? Then again, if I'd loved Connor as I should have, I wouldn't be standing here admiring the muscles in Creech's shoulders and wondering what it would feel like to run my hands over his back.

"Where's the nearest grocery? I need to go shopping." Creech went to the kitchen area and opened the fridge.

It took me a minute to register what he'd said, as I'd been lost in my thoughts. "There's a supermarket out on the highway, and a little place across from the condo complex, though it's on the pricey side."

Luckily, he hadn't caught on to the delay in my response, or maybe he just didn't ask where my thoughts had been. "I'd offer you a drink or food, but the best I can do is a glass of water. If I can find the glasses."

"How about I make you dinner?" It was out of my mouth before I could take it back. "I like to cook," I added. "My dad's a chef and he taught me a few tricks of the trade."

Creech raised his eyebrows. "You are a woman of many talents, Ms. Whitmeyer."

"A woman with a massive hunk of steak marinating in my fridge. It'll take me a week to eat the whole thing, I could use the help."

"I'd be happy to help you out, and I owe you for helping me move in." The dimple in his cheek was going to do me in. "What time would you like me over?"

I told him five and went home and hopped into the shower and then spent half an hour in front of my closet deciding what to wear, a choice of jeans or chinos, a red T-shirt or a blue one, before getting so annoyed with myself that I closed my eyes and grabbed, pulling out a pair of jeans and a pink shirt, and I told myself to just put it on already.

Creech looked like he'd cleaned up, wearing a chambray shirt rolled at the sleeves that showed off his corded forearms and a pair of jeans that accented his very fine backside. Again, I told myself to cut it out. We were neighbors, having a friendly dinner, nothing more. He had a bottle of red wine under his arm, which really didn't help with the friendly neighbor pretext.

He held the wine out. "As your coach, I shouldn't

be encouraging wine consumption, but it goes good with steak."

"You aren't officially my coach for a few weeks yet," I said, taking the wine and putting it on the counter separating the kitchen area from the great room. "Would you like the grand tour?"

"Will it take long?" he asked, deadpan.

Besides spending time stymied over what to wear, I had picked up the place. I began imagining what it looked like with fresh eyes, the Navaho blanket thrown over the back of my leather couch, the matching rug on the hardwood floor, the Georgia O'Keefe print over the fireplace. It was nice, I decided, and I was proud it was mine. "So, this is the main ballroom," I said standing in the living room. I pointed to the tile-topped high table by the counter. "The dining room is over there, and beyond, as you can see, is the kitchen." I went to the bedroom door. The last place I wanted to take him was into my bedroom, and so I stood at the threshold and pointed. "The master bedroom. Also, the only bedroom." I walked away quickly as I could manage, out the other door and onto the three season porch. "And, my favorite room."

Creech studied the wicker chairs, the small table between them, the shelf of books, and the view beyond the window of the butte that jutted out over the hills. "I can see why it's your favorite," he said.

"It's started to feel like home. It's nice to have a place to crash, with all the traveling we do."

"More home than Franconia?" he asked.

"I'm surprised you remember where I'm from."

Creech smirked. "Any fool who's watched the last four winter games knows where you're from, Mia."

I hadn't considered my partially famous state. I often forgot about it since celebrity wasn't an issue for me; it wasn't as if paparazzi were following me around. Having forgotten, I also felt a slight tinge of disappointment at his comment. "Want to sit out here? I can go open the wine and we can sip and enjoy the view while the steak cooks."

I went back to the kitchen, put the steak on to broil and tossed a quick salad and opened the wine, all the while questioning, again, what I was doing, inviting Creech to dinner.

I poured two glasses, went back to the porch, and handed him one. He looked like he belonged in the chair, admiring the view. "The place kind of grows on you. Park City, I mean," I said.

He took a sip. "I'd forgotten how glitzy it is, celebs and upscale housing. It's really different back where I'm from, I'd guess from Franconia, too. It's a little overwhelming."

I sat down in the other chair. "I don't imagine you're overwhelmed by much."

He gave me a questioning look. "I think you might be projecting there, Ice."

It felt funny to hear my nickname from him. "Why would you say that?"

He studied me for a minute. "Because you are the calmest, coolest, most collected woman I've ever met. It's what makes you a great racer."

"Ha. You don't know me very well, do you?" And then, before I spilled my guts on how unsteady I felt in his presence, how his sitting close enough to touch made me feel anything but cool and collected, I got up. "I should go see to the steak."

Creech

For a minute, maybe two, it seemed like I could have an easy, friendly relationship with Mia. She was funny and kind of sweet and I liked her, not just in the 'she makes my gut tighten' kind of way. Only problem was she did make my gut tighten. My thoughts kept tumbling to how soft her skin would be against mine, how gorgeous she'd be undressed. Not great friendly thoughts. We had history, a short and temporary romance, and we'd never slept together. Maybe that was the problem, the old unrequited love thing.

Here I was, sitting on her porch with the great view, sipping wine, listening to her in the kitchen. She was humming and it was the most endearing sound in the world and then I thought *God, you've got it bad, boy.* I got up and looked around, hoping for something else to pin my attention to. I found it on the bookshelf, right out in plain sight, the one thing that could slap me down like a bucket of cold water. There, in front of a shelf of novels, was a picture of Mia and her family. It looked like it was taken in a restaurant, and she had mentioned her parents owning one, her father the chef. A group of smiling people were gathered at a table. Mia, what must have been her mom and dad, another young man with his arm around an attractive dark haired girl. And a blond guy who looked like an Abercrombie and Fitch ad with his arm around Mia. I'd seen the guy before, in pictures if not in real life. I knew who he was.

Mia came back in and I put the picture, which I'd picked up to examine, back where I found it. "So, you're a snoop," she said.

I covered my embarrassment, which felt much larger than it ought. "Your family, right?"

She came over. "Yes. I love that shot, it was taken a few years ago at my family's restaurant. It's so seldom we're all together." She picked up the picture. "That's my brother, Sebastian and his wife, Jill and—" she stood staring.

"That's what's his name, Connor, right?" I don't know why I felt compelled to continue, but there it was.

"Yeah. I forgot he was in the picture." She put the photo back. "Dinner's ready."

I followed her inside, the picture bringing me back to Val D'Isere. The night we danced.

I wasn't going to follow Mia when she left so abruptly that night. I figured she must have her reasons and they were none of my business. But then, I figured it was maybe because of me she'd gone and I kept thinking about her in my arms and how bereft I felt when she'd left them, and me, empty. I sat at the table and sipped my beer, trying to join in the talk and the joking and thinking the whole time about her.

I got my jacket and said I was going to pack it in. It was a mile back to the hotel where we were staying, down a cobbled street and up a hill, at the base of the ski area. I had about a one in ten chance of catching up to her if I hurried and so I sprinted down the street, turned the corner to the hotel, and sure enough, there she was, walking along. "Mia, wait." I barely got the words out; the hard run had taken my breath.

She heard me, though, she turned and waited. I had no real plan about what I'd do once I caught up to her; I slowed to a walk so I could get my breath back. Her hair tossed around her long and loose and her cheeks were red with cold. "What's wrong?" she asked.

"Nothing," I said. And I put my hand to the back of her head and kissed her.

It was an impulsive thing to do, but it was the right thing and I could have stood in the cold all night long touching the silk of Mia's hair, her warm lips on mine, her fingers causing pinpricks down my spine as she caressed the back of my neck.

When we finally came apart, she held me in those eyes so much like a clear blue sky. "Is that what you ran up here to tell me?"

I took her hand and drew a circle on her palm. "Pretty much."

"It's cold. We should go in."

"Yes, we should." We walked the rest of the way up to the hotel hand in hand.

I walked her to her room, which was just down the hall from my own, a nervous energy coursing through me and threatening to set me off like a rocket.

"Melissa's still at the club," she said, unlocking her door. Melissa was her roommate and I knew, without her saying anything more, we would spend the night together and it made me so happy I felt like I'd grown wings.

She put the do not disturb sign on the door before shutting us inside and taking off her coat. I took off my jacket while, in my mind's eye, I undressed her. She was so beautiful, tall and graceful and perfect.

We sat down on the bed. "You want a soda or something?" she asked.

I pulled my fingers though her hair. "What I want is to kiss you again."

"Okay."

We lay down together. Despite the lightning coursing through me and the hard-on I was sure she could feel through both my jeans and hers, a quiet voice in my head told me to take it slow. Maybe it was the way her fingers stroked along the side of my face or the way she felt underneath me, like we were two pages in a book, but I felt this incredible tenderness toward her, as though what we had here was a fragile thing, an easy thing to mess up.

We lay there for a long time, kissing and stroking and pretty much lost in one another. It was when we finally came up for air that I noticed it, the picture on the nightstand. In it Mia was in a blue dress, flowers in her hair. And, in a tux, with his arm around her waist, was the guy, Connor. He was staring straight at me as though to say, "She's mine, man. Leave her alone."

I wanted her about as much as a parched man wanted water, but I couldn't ignore what the guy was telling me. She wasn't mine to have and I knew, in that flash second epiphany, I knew she wasn't a girl to just fool around with. If I did, she would feel guilty about it and then she'd hate me. I got up off the bed.

"What's wrong?" she asked.

"I don't want to do anything we'll both regret later." I put on my jacket, hoping all the while she'd tell me I was wrong, she'd stop me and talk me into staying the night.

She sat up on the bed, her eyes so sad it broke my heart. "Then I guess you'd better go."

Mia

Connor had been family, as much as my brother and Jill and my mom and dad, so much a part of my family and my life I'd forgotten he was in the picture. He'd always been in the picture. Until he wasn't. I don't know which bothered me more, the fact he wasn't family anymore or the fact I'd forgotten he was in the photo I displayed so prominently on my bookcase.

I busied myself with getting the steak from the broiler, mixing oil and vinegar for the salad. Maybe I could still get through this. Though as we sat down to our simple meal, Creech avoided my eyes as though he'd seen me naked. Maybe he had—not naked, exactly, but vulnerable.

"This is terrific," he said, concentrating on his steak as though cutting it was a life or death matter.

"Thank you."

We worked our way through dinner with stilted conversation and, as he helped me stack dishes into the dishwasher, I made a choice. I could keep it like this, our relationship like near strangers meeting in the street, or I could be straightforward. "The photo on my bookshelf," I said. "I forgot Connor was in it."

"You mentioned that," Creech ran his fingers over his empty wine glass.

"More wine?"

He put the glass on the counter. "I think I've had enough. I should probably get going."

"Connor and I broke up over the summer. We'd been together since high school." I gathered the wine glasses and brought them to the sink, mostly for something to do and at least my back was to him, so he wouldn't see me cry. "It was for the best, you know? But it's still, there's this space where..." I took a deep breath. "I don't know why I'm telling you this."

He came over to me and stroked the back of my

neck. "I'm glad you did, tell me."

God, his hand in my hair set me on fire. "You ever think about us, about that time, a long time ago?" I was thinking about it now. How he'd kissed me in a way that made the whole world disappear. How I thought then Connor had never kissed me like that, how it was still true.

"Yes, I think about it. Meeting you again has brought it all back. I think about what crappy timing I had where you were concerned."

"We've still got crappy timing, huh?"

His fingers grazed my chin and he looked into my eyes. "The crappiest." We stood there like that for a moment. Then he let go. "I should go home."

"Before we do something we'll regret?" I asked, which got a sad smile from him.

"Night, Mia." He stopped at the door. "For the record? That night in Val D'Isere? I wish to God I'd stayed."

Six

Mia

I shouldn't have let him leave with that line still fluttering in the air. But I did. I guess I was being a coward, afraid of what would happen if I called him on it. Afraid of how he'd answer me; if he'd turned around, come back to me, and kissed me I would have gone over the edge.

If I was lucky, I had a few good years left on the circuit. I wasn't about to get sidelined like Tinny had. Creech as my coach would be enough of an adjustment without my doing something stupid, like falling into bed with him. I fell into my bed alone that night and tossed around, Val D'Isere on an endless film loop in my head. Each time the film played, I'd give it a different ending. The ending I liked best was the one where Creech didn't make a speech about regrets.

By morning I was angry at myself for not having confronted him. I was angry at him, too, for leaving his regret unanswered in the airspace between us. My life was turbulent enough; I didn't need my ancient history with Creech Crèches churning me around like a washing machine agitator.

I got ready for a jog and then, instead of turning left to go to the trailhead, I turned right to go to Creech's condo. I would knock on the door and ask him what the hell he'd been thinking. I thought we were clear, we were supposed to be friends and nothing but.

There was a large U-haul parked by the curb of his building's entrance. Out of the back, cradling a dresser drawer in his arms, jumped a man who looked familiar. His hair was lighter and he was shorter and more muscular, but the resemblance to Creech was unmistakable. I held the door for him and we both made our way up the stairs, where Creech's door stood open.

He looked at me surprised when I followed him into the apartment. "You the girl next door?" he asked.

"Close. I live a few buildings down. I popped in to see Creech."

His eyebrows went up as he looked me over. "He always gets the pretty girls." Then he stopped. "Hey, wait a minute. Are you Mia Whitmeyer?"

"I was last I looked."

"Holy crap. I'm a big fan. I follow women's skiing—with my brother coaching and all." He stacked the drawer on top of several others. "Sorry, forgot my manners. I'm Eric, Creech's younger, handsomer, and more charming brother. Also smarter." He grinned and offered up his hand. "Although since he talked me into driving his possessions clear across the country, the smarter might be questionable."

"I hope you were fairly compensated." I shook his hand.

"I wasn't until now."

Creech came out of the bedroom. "Is the rest of the bed frame still on the—" He noticed me and stopped dead. "Mia, good morning. I see you've met Eric."

"Yes, I've had the pleasure," Eric said.

"Quit ogling, man." Creech turned to me. "Pardon him, he's hopeless."

There was nowhere to go but small talk, I followed Creech's lead. "Your furniture got here quick."

"Yeah, my brothers drive like maniacs. Adam, the other brother, went to hunt down coffee. I told him about the little market across the street. He should have been back by now, maybe he took my truck and left town."

"Nice of them to help you out."

"They work cheap. I have to put up with them for the rest of the week. Okay, maybe not so cheap."

"Personally, I'm in it for the adventure. And then

there's the added bonus of meeting celebrities like yourself," Eric said.

I liked Eric; he seemed like a big kid. "You guys live back east?"

"I do, I moved back to Wells, somebody's got to keep the family legacy."

"Eric is going to run the family ski area," Creech said.

"Your family has a ski area?"

"Yup. They're part owners of Ridge Run, one of the few remaining Mom and Pop areas left in the Adirondacks, or anywhere, for that matter. Did I never tell you that?" Creech asked.

"Why would you have told her that?" Eric asked.

"Mia and I used to know each other, way back when I was on the circuit." Creech looked at me like those words were a loaded shotgun. Maybe they were.

"And your other brother?" I asked changing the subject.

"Lives right around the corner. In Alta. He's ski patrol, avalanche control."

"Interesting."

"I'm sure he'd be happy to tell you all about it," said Creech. "Anyhow, you come by to help move furniture?"

"No." I stood there for a minute, needing an excuse for why I had come by. Our timing was still crappy. "I was going to show you where the trailhead was, you know the one down behind the complex."

"The one where you were attacked by brambles?" Creech asked.

A third man appeared at the door. There was no mistaking him for Creech's brother, the two looked so much alike they might have been twins, except the brother was a little taller and thinner and his hair was longer. He held out a tray of coffees. "I would have brought extras if I knew you were having company," he said. He put the tray on the counter. "You look familiar," he said to me.

"Adam, Mia Whitmeyer. Mia, my brother, Adam," Creech said by way of introduction.

"*The* Mia Whitmeyer? Fastest woman to ever ski down a hill Mia Whitmeyer?"

Creech sighed. "Pardon my brothers. I don't know where my parents went wrong."

"I can go get more coffee," said Adam.

I looked from brother, to brother, to brother. "That's okay, I should get going. Nice to meet you guys. Enjoy your visit."

Creech

I doubted Mia had stopped by to show me the jogging trail. And I doubted it was to announce her undying love.

My brothers were, both of them, grinning ear to ear. Eric handed me a cup. "We have much to learn from you, oh wise elder one."

"Mia and I knew each other, you know, a long time ago," mimed Adam. "Who else you been hiding from us?"

"I'm her coach."

"Yep." Eric raised his eyebrows. "So what you coaching her to do?"

I raised my own brows. "Wouldn't you like to know?" We drank the coffee and emptied the truck. Despite the teasing where Mia was concerned, it was great to have my brothers here. They were good guys, all in all, and they had offered to haul my furniture across the country, so I owed them at least a few days of time as they explored my new digs in Park City. Eric talked about coming back in ski season and Adam said he could drop in and keep an eye on me, now that I lived nearby.

My brothers got the message; Mia was a member of the team I was coaching who happened to live in my condo complex. I was glad to let it rest, because the truth was I'd spent half the night thinking about her and hoped to God my feelings weren't written on my sleeve.

I might have known Adam would bring it up again. Truck unloaded, furniture unpacked and set up, we put my grill together on the balcony and went to the market for some hamburgers and macaroni salad and beer. After dinner, we watched the Broncos on Sunday night NFL on my newly hooked up TV.

I had two bedrooms and two beds, so Adam and Eric tossed a coin to see who'd get the bed and who would have to sleep on the couch. Eric won the toss and, since he'd driven the last leg of the journey while Adam slept, he went to bed at halftime.

I got the last two Millers from the fridge and handed one to Adam. He took the beer, considered it for a minute and asked, "How well do you know Mia Whitmeyer?"

"Why, you plan on asking her out?"

"I'm not sure you'd want me to do that, not that I need your permission. I hope, at least, she's available, for your sake? No attachments?" The beer must have loosened his tongue. There was some uneasiness between us still, having to do with my ex-girlfriend, Mallory Prescott. Mallory and I have remained friends, she lived in Lake Placid near where I was coaching, and last year, when Adam had come to visit, he'd made a play for her. This despite the fact that she was living with a guy and had a kid with him.

I know Mallory about as well as I know myself, and I knew it wasn't like her to invite his advances. I know my brother really well, too. He'd had a crush on Mallory since forever and he'd acted like a jerk. We'd had a huge fight about it and made up with an uneasy peace afterward. He was my brother, and the fact he'd been willing to haul my stuff across the country went a long way to making amends.

"If that's your slick way of asking me about Mallo," I said to him. "She's happy and I'm happy for her." Mallory and her boyfriend, extreme skier PD Bell, had gotten married a few weeks before I left for points west. They'd had a small ceremony on the summit of Whiteface Mountain. Their little girl, Emily, was flower girl and I acted as best man. "And besides," I added, pointing my beer bottle towards the empty white walls of my new condo, "I've got a whole new life now."

Adam settled back on the couch. "You do have a sweet job. You don't perchance need an assistant, do you? And I don't plan on making a play for Mia, you have my word on it."

I gave him a smirk. "Your word?"

"I'm reformed." He smiled brightly. "Anyway, I think she's into you."

"She's not into me. She lives a few doors down and I'm her coach. End of story."

"Whatever you say, brother." We watched the second half of the game and it wasn't mentioned again.

Mia

Reni and Rachel came into Park City a few nights after Creech's brothers, which offered me another diversion from my thoughts. Although Tinny was and had been my best friend, I loved these two. Rachel with her fun and wildness, Reni with her soft serious nature, were great friends to share the travel-heavy life we lead. When they arrived, I offered up my place for a girl's night, I'd make fish tacos and we'd drink a few margaritas, a sort of Mardi Gras before having to go back to the strict diet and training regimen racing required of us.

We toasted the upcoming season and Rachel entertained us with stories of her exploits off-season, where she'd managed to date four guys at the same time. Reni was from back east, like me, and we compared notes about the goings on in our respective homes, hers in Middlebury, Vermont and mine over the New Hampshire border in Franconia. She also had a new man in her life, a graduate student at Middlebury College, and she was bubbling over with details about him.

After a while, we got around to talking about Tinny. "I can't believe it," Rachel said. "She hasn't been with the guy for all that long."

"Since last year," I said. "They are unbearably cute together."

Reni took a sip of her drink. "When it's right, you know it. Doesn't take long to figure it out."

"This Paul guy's got your head spinning, girl." Rachel looked at her glass. "I need a refill."

"I'll make another round." I went to the kitchen and began putting stuff in the blender. "Reni's right. They're in love, anyone can see it."

"You relationship people are killing me," said Rachel. "How long you and Connor O' Hottie been together, Ice? Since the dawn of time?"

I concentrated on the blender button. It whirred loudly, and I swallowed hard. Maybe someday it would get easier to talk about it. I hoped that day came soon. "We broke up," I said once I'd silenced the noise.

Reni nearly dropped her glass. "You what?"

I shrugged and poured another round. "Actually, he dumped me. Waiting too long was a bad idea."

I took a sip of the margarita. I didn't really believe it would help and I'd be a mess come morning, but I didn't much care.

"Jeez, honey, you want to talk about it?" Reni asked.

I shrugged. "I'll be fine. It's just you know, Coach gone and Tin leaving and Connor." Despite my best efforts, I started to tear up.

"Hey," Reni put an arm around me. "It'll get better, you'll see."

Rachel handed me a tissue. "Look at all you've got going on, Mia. I'm jealous as hell of what you can do out on the hill. You've got a better chance than any of us of taking another World Cup title. And if the whole racing thing doesn't work out for you, you can come be my personal chef."

I smiled. "Thanks, guys. I live to beat you down the hill. And make you margaritas."

"Maybe Connor wasn't the right guy," Reni said softly.

"It's kind of shitty of him, to wait all that time and then decide he'd had enough. A lot of guys would cut off their right arms for a chance with you," Rachel added.

I hugged them both. "This is why I love you guys. If I plan some ex-girlfriend revenge, like sugar in his gas tank, you're on board, right?"

"Oh yes. I loves me some revenge." Rachel gave me a squeeze.

"The best revenge would be your happiness. We need to find you a new man," said Reni. She looked sort of half serious.

"I don't think I'm ready for a new man just yet."

"You can be my wing woman," said Rachel. "We'll date every guy in Europe. Meanwhile, we got the world's hottest coach. I could watch his cute ass all day long. And I can do it without getting a restraining order." She raised her eyebrows.

"He is pretty," added Reni. "He's also a really terrific coach, he's one of the reasons I'm here."

"He was your coach in development, right?" asked Rachel.

"Yup. All the girls had major crushes on him. He's kind of a serial dater from what I hear. The guy gets around."

"He's a flirt," I said, "but he's more serious than you might think. He's a really good guy."

They both looked at me with eyebrows raised. "You surprise me, Ice. I didn't think you were a fast worker," Rachel said.

I felt my face go hot, a nice combination, tear stained and blushing. "I knew him, back in his racing days."

"You knew him?" Rachel repeated.

"He used to be pretty good, right?" Reni said. "Then he had some really bad accident in a training run and it ruined his racing career."

"He was one of the top skiers on the men's team, back when I first came up. It was a long time ago. He flirted a lot, but he didn't seem to mean it. He had this ex-girlfriend I think he was still hung up on."

"Mallory," said Reni and it was my turn to raise my eyebrows.

"She was on patrol at Whiteface when I raced there in development," Reni continued. "And back in the day, she was big on the college circuit. She and Coach Creech were friends, or so he said. I always thought it was a little weird he had a woman as his best bud. But she lived, probably still does, with PD Bell. They have a kid together"

"PD Bell, the extreme skier?" asked Rachel. "God, he's another hottie. An amazing skier and scary wild. He makes racing look like a Sunday stroll in the park."

"What, running your skis down the fall line at eighty miles per isn't wild enough for you, darling?" I teased. Rachel was the most fearless of us. It was little wonder she specialized in downhill, the fastest of our events, which might be described as point your skis down the hill and go.

"He skied down the West Rib of Denali last year. First you have to climb up and then you ski down. It's pretty radical." Rachel raised her glass. "Maybe after I quit racing, I'll give it a try."

"You would. Too bad Bell's taken. He'd be perfect for you," Reni said. "But anyway, if Creech was holding a torch for Mallory Prescott, I'd guess he got himself burned."

Seven

In October, I threw myself into conditioning for the season. I told myself I needed to, and this was true—a lot of the girls I was competing with were ten years younger than me. I wasn't exactly over the hill, but I needed to work to stay at the top of my game. Training was also a way to keep my thoughts from straying into mull territory. I had a lot to mull about, most of it had to do with my new coach, and I really didn't want to go there. At night, I fell into bed too tired to dream, let alone ruminate.

Late in the month, we went to Copper Mountain in Colorado for a few exhibition races. The high altitude at the resort would assure some snow cover, even so early in the season, or so those who planned the event thought. Turned out, the weather was in the forties with intermittent rain sputtering though the cloud cover. Too warm for snowmaking, they had to truck in the snow. Even so, the downhill, which required a longer course, was cancelled.

Tinny, who lived a few hours' drive from the resort, came up for the meet. She looked pale, which she said was because she was still throwing up a lot. And she looked a little sad. I knew she probably wanted more than anything to get out on the course and it was killing her that she couldn't do it. I had, as we all did, several dozen pairs of skis that traveled with me. We had ski technicians to advise us as to what works best, given course and conditions, and I trusted them. If only to get Tinny out of her funk, I asked her advice as well. She looked at me as though I'd grown two heads and suggested going shorter and softer for the sloppy conditions, which was exactly what the techs had said.

"I've got some new Atomics I'd like to try," I told her.

"I've never had good luck with their stuff. I don't have your strength," she offered.

"It's a good time to try them, before Europe. See if I'll add them." My favorites were a pair of Blizzard skis made of titanium and wood, but they were stiff and unforgiving, great for speed but not for the mush we'd be facing in these races.

"Why not? You don't have anything to prove here. Besides, this isn't the kind of hard junk you love so much," she said with a smirk. It was good to have her back, if only for a moment.

She was right; it was just an exhibition, a chance to get out on the snow, a warm up for the season to come. Officially, the meet would be used to help determine who ended up at which level, but for me and Rachel and Reni, it was little more than a formality. Our standings in last year's World Cup alone would keep us on top, even if we didn't ski well here. It was a done deal for Cara and Lara too, unless several women from below pulled off scorching runs, they were part of the team. The only real question was who would fill Tin's spot. All the girls on B and a few on C had a good shot. It was anybody's guess who would get the nod. I could imagine, too, that being replaced was going to be hard for Tin to watch, because she would be thinking it wouldn't be so easy to come back. It would be hard for me to watch her replacement, though I would do everything I could to help the new girl fit in. Skiing was an individual sport, but we were also a team, representing our country in world events, and it was important we acted like a team. I'd always liked my team members. Or, at the very least, I respected and tolerated them.

The downhill was cancelled and so was the combined, a one-two combination of downhill and slalom, which were at two ends of the ski racing spectrum. While downhill was about straight-out no-holds-barred speed, the slalom involved turning through a line of gates, and split second timing was key. Left up for contest was the super G, the giant slalom-GS event, and the slalom. They would be run over three days, with women racing in the morning and men in the afternoon.

The first race day, the Super G event, turned out brighter than predicted. The sun poked through the clouds and it was one of those fall days warm enough for shirt sleeves. Super G had always been my best event. With wide gates, it was a hybrid between downhill and slalom, requiring some technical turns but also a lot of out and out speed.

We drew for start slots and I drew an early start, second to race right behind Lara Brandt. In these conditions, early could be an advantage. The soft snow was carved easily into moguls and ruts, much the way a Jeep can cut deep tire marks into a muddy dirt road, and those ruts would be challenging for later racers. The trouble with an early start was that the snow itself was heavy and carving through it felt a lot like carving through wet cement. I was a power skier, being six feet tall and muscular served me well in situations like this one. I'd run a similar course in a race at Copper the year before and, since the conditions had been close to perfect on that day, I had set a record time. I was nowhere near that time on this day, a full three seconds slower, which, in a race where winning was often a matter of a few hundredths of a second, was turtle slow. It was faster though, than the time Lara set down and as the two of us stood at the bottom of the hill and watched the other racers come down, it became more and more apparent that the time would be enough for a win.

Creech was at the top of the hill and skied down after the race to congratulate me. We had kept up the coach-racer relationship pretty well during training, and I hadn't again mentioned our dinner. Neither had he. Maybe it was coming from him, or maybe it was that I wasn't happy with the lousy time I'd set, but his congratulations rubbed me the wrong way.

"Nothing to write home about," I said, pulling off my helmet.

"You pushed it enough to win. Though I get that good enough isn't part of your vocabulary."

"Because it wasn't good enough," I said. "The entire Austrian team would be able to beat it, as could a whole lot of the other women on FIS."

"You did what you had to do. If the Austrians were here, you would have pushed harder."

"I should have pushed harder anyway." I knew I was being obstinate. If I being were honest, I knew my being obstinate had nothing to do with my skiing. Creech seemed to know better than to argue anymore.

"Go have lunch with Tin. You'll feel better," he said before leaving me to stew.

Racing went from bad to worse after that. The giant slalom, GS, was the next day. It was usually a great event for me, like super G only with gates closer together to require more turns. The weather was increasingly awful. It was still warm, but clouds had moved in and started squeezing drizzle over the course, and the top of the run was shrouded in a dense fog that stuck to my racing suit and beaded on my goggles, making it hard to see.

I drew the fifth start. Reni was just ahead of me, and she radioed back up to the top to say the course was rutted, but doable if you didn't mind skiing blind through the first two thirds of it.

"You make it sound so fun," I said.

"We've seen worse." She went over the course with me. "Watch out for the rut at gate four. It's extra sucky, and water skis would come in handy, there's a puddle forming at the finish."

"You heard her," Creech said as I headed for the start gate. "You've seen worse. Do what you've got to and don't sweat the rest."

Again, his advice, though it was exactly what any

coach would have said, grated. I chased it from my head as I took my place and the count to start began. I could do this by rote, the beep, the feel of the start bar against my shins and I was off. It was like skiing through ether. I had the course in my head and I let instinct take over, still I had to slow more than I liked.

Then the sun decided to come out, like a spotlight, right at the gate Reni had pegged as troublesome. If I could barely see before, I was blinded now. My skis clattered through the gate and the left ski climbed up the rut and sent me off balance. I had slowed, but I was still going at a pretty good speed, and now I had to put the brakes on and fight to keep my balance and make my way through three more gates to the finish. I managed to get control quickly, but in doing it I tourqued my knee at an awkward angle, and by the time I straightened and flew right, I knew I might have done some damage.

I managed to finish the race, though my time wasn't great, it was a tenth of a second behind Reni, who held the top spot. My knee hurt and I took off my skis and walked around the finish area a few times, relieved that I could still walk and hoping I hadn't done any real damage.

Tin and Reni joined me at the bottom. "You okay?" Tin asked.

"I wrenched my knee on four," I said. "It's not too bad. I think I'm fine."

I radioed up and gave my report. "You okay?" Creech got on the radio and asked Tin's question all over again. "I hear you had a near miss."

"I'm fine," I repeated, though my knee still barked when I walked.

"You posted real well, considering," he said.

"Reni posted better," I said, before signing off. Then I wondered why I was being such a brat.

The other racers came down; none of them beat Reni or me. Until Mary Tyco came along. She was brand new, she'd been one of Creech's racers at the development levels and she'd done so well they advanced her to D team. She flew down the course and beat Reni by a solid tenth of a second. True, it was sunny by then and visibility was a lot better than it had been when Reni and I raced. But, conditions aside, it was an impressive run, particularly for a rookie.

I went up to congratulate her. She was seventeen, about the same age as I had been when I came up, and I remembered how overwhelmed I'd felt. If I could do anything to ease her in, I'd be happy to do it. She looked at me, and instead of saying thanks, said, "Better get used to it. I'm younger and faster than you." And she walked away. I stood shaking my head, not sure whether to be angry or to laugh.

"What a little shit," said Tin, who'd overheard. Which pretty much summed up what I was feeling.

My knee stopped creaking once I changed from ski boots into sneakers. As much as I loved to ski, and as much as my boots fit me to perfection, it was an amazing feeling to pull them off. Even the heaviest of snow boots felt like bedroom slippers in comparison. I jogged around in my sneaks, jumped up and down a few times, and was happy that my knee didn't scream at me. Still, I knew better than to take a knee strain lightly and so I went to see the trainer, Lance Monroe.

I sat down on the bench and Lance sat in front of me. Pulling the sneaker off, he put my foot on his thigh and began prodding my knee working his fingers down my calf to my ankle. "Any pain?"

"No, just a little twinge here," I pointed to the knee joint.

"Doesn't look like anything serious, but we should still get an MRI when we get back to Park City."

Creech had come into the training room. He sat down next to Lance. "You sure it's okay?"

"See for yourself," said Lance, moving over so Creech could get in front of me. He took my foot up into his lap and I held my breath. His fingers were long and sturdy and though he went through the same motions

Lance had, all I could imagine was those fingers traveling up my thighs. I nearly shook my head as I told myself to cut it out.

"It doesn't hurt?" His eyes met mine and cutting it out got a lot harder. He was just being a concerned coach, but my libido didn't want to believe that.

"It doesn't hurt."

Thankfully, he let go of my leg, though my foot was still in his lap. "Getting an MRI is a good idea," he said. I nodded. "And I'm pulling you from the slalom tomorrow."

I took my leg off of his lap. "What?"

Creech stood up. "I don't want to take any stupid chances."

I got up and we stood toe to toe. "You just heard Lance tell you the knee is fine. You heard me say it didn't hurt."

Lance raised his hands. "I think Creech might be right, if it's not necessary, don't do it." And with that, he walked out the door.

"Since when is racing an unnecessary risk?" I asked.

Creech frowned, a furrow in his brow. "You don't need the race, you don't have anything to prove here. We have our first international meet in a couple of weeks and I need you healthy. So you're off the roster tomorrow. End of story. Don't make this harder than it should be."

"Everything about working with you is harder than it should be." I grabbed my sneaker and hobbled, one shoe off, one on, out the door.

Creech

I watched her leave, feeling totally exasperated and knowing full well no other woman, on this team or any other, would have had the same effect on me. Mia hated not being able to race, but had Lance suggested she be sidelined, as he probably would have if I hadn't gotten into the middle of it, she would have accepted it without much more than a disapproving frown.

We would have to figure out what was going on between us, but here and now wasn't the place to do it. Let her simmer, she'd get over it. Since the next day came up rainy again, I figured she'd be happy not to have to deal with the slop on the course.

The slalom is run through sets of flagged gates that marked the turns. Miss a gate, and the skier is disqualified. Racers have to memorize the gates as they climb to the start house. The race is run twice, with different gate patterns for each run. I set the gates for the first run, and because the weather was so bad, I made the gates less challenging than I might have in better conditions. Any junior racer could have run them without trouble in good weather, and these women were far better than junior racers.

I caught sight of Mia, standing in her rain gear with Tinny Renton at the finish. I waved but she either didn't see me or pretended not to notice. I chose to believe it was the former, and I was glad she'd come out to support the other racers, though really, I had known all along she would.

The rain beat down and we tried to get the skiers in and out of the start as quickly as we could. Despite the relatively simple gate set, about half of the racers missed gates and were disqualified. At the end of the first run, Reni Auckland was in first place, with Lara Brandt a few hundredths of a second behind her, no surprise as both women were slalom specialists. Rachel King was in third, which was good for her as she was more of a down-hiller and slalom had never been a great event for her. In fourth was Mary Tyco, an excellent run for a rookie in her first race with the big girls.

The second course was set by Davey Delacroix, one of the assistant coaches. The rain had let up and he set a more challenging course. Reni missed a gate near the top, and then Rachel missed the same gate. Lara, aware of the problem, skied more cautiously than she might have, but still had enough to hold on to the top spot. And Mary skied well enough to grab second place.

We had a meeting to decide official team standings after the meet. It was little more than a formality for the most part, the five women on the A team last year would get their spots back. But the sixth spot was wide open.

Mike Granberg was head of US racing and his word carried clout. He'd seen Mary Tyco race and he was duly impressed. It was little wonder he advised we give the spot to her.

I had to admit she was impressive. But I did have a few concerns. "She's a phenom, no doubt about it, but she's awfully green. Maybe it would be better if she got a couple of FIS races under her skis first."

Mike considered. "Mary reminds me of Mia Whitmeyer, when she first came up. She went to A team her first year. It's worked out pretty well for all of us."

"Yeah, but Mia did have a few races before they moved her up, later in the season, as I recall." What I didn't add was that Mia, even Mia at eighteen, was nothing like Mary once you got past the skiing talent. But then, I wasn't sure if I was looking through some sort of hazy nostalgic mirror or it I was remembering her clearly. And comparing the twenty-nine year old Mia to Mary Tyco was hardly fair to Mary, who had neither the experience nor the maturity Mia had now.

Mike put his hand to my shoulder. "I trust you to take her under your wing. You know her, you coached her in development and that's a tremendous advantage. I think we'd be doing her and the team a disservice if we didn't go with her after what she showed here."

I did know Mary, I knew she was temperamental and moody, even for a teenager. Yes, she had tremendous talent, but she wasn't ice and fire, she wasn't Mia Whitmeyer, and I had to wonder if she'd burn out long before she became a superstar.

Eight

Mia

My knee was MRIed and prodded at the training center and, much as I suspected, there was nothing wrong with it. I had a notion to go to Creech and say I told you so. I hadn't said anything to him since our run-in in the training room. The emotional tumult I'd felt by just letting him poke my knee joint reaffirmed my decision—I would keep my distance, as much as possible with him as coach, because getting close to him would mean taking a plunge I wasn't ready for and couldn't afford to take.

Mary Tyco was given Tinny's spot on the team and this nearly made me break my vow. In my most humble opinion, little Mary might have scorched the competition at junior levels, but she wasn't seasoned enough to replace Tinny, even if she had a good outing at Copper. I wanted to ask Creech what he thought he was doing. Then again, my first impression of Mary hadn't been good and maybe I needed to cut her some slack.

"They've taken her on as your replacement," Reni teased as she and Rachel and Cara and I had lunch together.

I told them of my run-in with her after the GS. "Tinny called her a little shit. Maybe I'm being too harsh, maybe she was just nervous."

"Probably she was nervous." Cara picked at her salad. "We can all say dumb things under pressure. And it was her first time." I couldn't imagine Cara trash talking anyone, not even under pressure.

"She's probably a little shit," Rachel said. "She raced after me in the slalom, and I swear to God, she sneered at me at the finish." She picked up her water. "I should take her out on the town. Get her drunk." She smiled wickedly.

"Creech would have you for lunch if you do that," Reni said. "He's pretty protective of her. I think he's worried because she's so young."

"She is young," I agreed. I can't say I much liked the idea of Creech being her knight in shining armor.

We began the official FIS season close to home that year, at Beaver Creek in Colorado. From there, we would go to Whistler, in the Canadian Rockies, then Waterville Valley, back east near my home town, which meant I could take a few days at Christmas to visit with my family. After the holiday, we were off to Europe, where we would stay for the next three months. There were a lot of races, and when we weren't racing, we were training. Any crazy romantic notions I had about Creech Crèches, or any other guy, would have to be kept in the fantasy department as I chased down another World Cup title.

The western meets went well for everyone except Mary Tyco. As I had suspected, she was too green, and she folded when the competition got tougher. And it was tough. All of the European teams and the Canadians had at least a couple of women who could win on any given day. The Austrians were a powerhouse, led by Katya Hofstadter, the only woman who'd been racing FIS as long as I had. We had a long-standing competition going, Katya and I. She took best overall at Beaver Creek, and I grabbed it back from her at Whistler.

Katya may have been my nemesis, but I respected her as a racer and I liked her as a woman. We chatted amiably at the finish of the downhill at Whistler, as Rachel came flying down the hill to beat us both.

"You have a nice new coach," she said, her English much better than my halting German. "Toll," she added, using the German word for great with a wink.

"Toll ist wahr," I said, agreeing with her in my very bad German accent, which made her laugh. Katya had gotten married last summer. Her new husband was also her personal trainer. "Congratulations on your... I searched for right word. "Neuer Mann." This made her laugh some more.

"Thank you. I like my new man, is nice to married be."

"Hans Jorgen travels with you, you must really like him," I teased. As I thought of the lanky blond Austrian in the start house, I couldn't help thinking of Creech.

Mary Tyco had just come streaking into the finish, to a disappointing thirtieth. She looked so dejected as she glanced at the leader board that I felt sorry for her. It was hard coming up from junior levels, I remembered it well enough. And she was good, by next season she'd start winning races, maybe she would replace me eventually, who knew? I decided I'd try to be good to her, help her if I could. Even if she was a little shit.

I sat next to Mary on the plane ride east. "It'll get easier," I told her. My comment drew a cold hard stare. I tried again. "You've got a ton of talent. It takes time, adjusting. I remember when I first came up, it took a while. You're going to be great."

Her stare was still fastened on me. "I'm not you. I'm going to be better than you. Better than the bony-assed Austrian you're so friendly with." She raised her eyebrows as though she wanted a fight.

"Listen up, baby girl. You've got a lot to learn and you ain't there yet. What you get, you earn. Come talk to me in about ten years, if you're still around. Which, if you don't change your attitude, you won't be. And by the way, that bony-assed Austrian can ski rings around your little fanny, so a bit of respect might be in order."

The only empty seat was next to Creech, across the aisle. I considered my options and then got up and moved. It was a small plane and everyone, including the coaches, had overheard. "Not a word," I said, as I sat down.

"Didn't say a thing," he muttered under his breath.

I drew a later start, fifteen, for the downhill at Waterville Valley. The hill was perfect, new snow had added to snowmaking and there was just a whisper of powder over a solid surface. Creech came up to me in the start house. "Listen, I know Mary Tyco irritates the crap out you. Just don't let it get to you, okay? You're still the best we got."

I nearly laughed at him. "Mary is a pain in the ass, but a problem she isn't." I didn't add that he was the bigger problem for me, that his standing close to me was a problem, that his brushing my arm was keeping me from concentrating. "It's all good," I said, pasting on a smile. Then I walked away and plugged into my iPod. I liked isolating myself before a meet, and I had Nirvana and Pearl Jam cued up to blast into my ears to get me into race mode.

By my start, I was in a good place. Creech may have said something, I didn't hear him. The point was to follow the fall line, let out as much speed as I could without crashing, and devour the hill. I had a great run. I knew it even before I looked up to the leader board, which confirmed it. I was in first, half a second ahead of Katya and a full second ahead of Rachel in third. I waved to my parents, who watched from the sidelines, my mother shook cowbells and my dad gave me a thumbs up. I waited as the rest of the racers came down, none of them got close to Rachel let alone me. Mary Tyco skied a full four seconds behind me, enough for oblivion place or so and I did an inward gloat and then told myself I needed to be more mature than that.

Creech skied down after the race to congratulate me. I introduced him to my parents.

"So you're the new guy," said my dad. "Tough to

fill Marv's shoes, I'd guess."

"I wouldn't even try." Creech put his hand to my shoulder. "Mia makes my job easy." It was a nice thing to say, but the hand on the shoulder made me want to lean into him and put my head against his chest, a reflex move I countered by taking a small step away from him and reminding myself he was a decent coach and he was just doing his job. Creech, for his part, took his hand away before my parents could notice anything amiss.

The meet ended on the twenty third of December, and I wasn't expected in Cortina until the end of the month, so I took the few days over Christmas off to spend the holiday with my parents in Franconia.

My brother and sister-in-law wouldn't be coming this year, but my folks invited some of their friends and relatives who lived locally to Christmas dinner, though Christmas Eve would be just the three of us. I spent a morning cooking with my father; he made a beef bourguignon for Christmas Eve while I did a sausage and ricotta stuffing for the Christmas turkey. We worked alongside companionably. My dad wasn't much of a talker, which was fine with me. Talking would lead to a discussion about skiing, which might lead back to Creech and he was taking up enough space in my thoughts. He had gone home to the Adirondacks and I imagined him at family dinner with his brothers and parents and I wondered what it would be like to join them and then wondered why I'd think about it at all.

Despite my mother breezing in and out to taste our creations as she did last minute decorating and cleaning, and despite my father's congenial quiet, I sensed there was something wrong. As we sat down to Christmas Eve dinner, the sense became stronger.

"We're sorry we didn't make Coach Marv's memorial," my Dad said. "He was a great guy." Maybe that was it, my parents were examining their own aging. Coach Marv had been only a few years older than my dad and was probably an unpleasant reminder of mortality. The thought brought a lump to my throat. I swallowed it down with Cabernet.

"I miss him," I said. "I hear him in my head sometimes, as I'm standing at the start. He used to say 'you're bigger than the hill, now go get it' before races." I smiled as I wiped away a tear.

My mom put her hand on top of mine. "I'm sure he's still with you, with all the girls."

I closed my eyes for a moment as my dad said, "The new coach seems good. Much younger than I thought he'd be."

"He's about my age," I said. "I actually knew him as a racer; he was on the circuit when I started out."

"No kidding," said my dad.

"I'm an old lady by circuit standards," I joked.

My mom took my quip more seriously. "You can do anything you set your mind to—the world's wide open when you retire." She laughed. "Listen to me, talking to my daughter about retirement."

"I'm not quite there yet," I said. "I plan on Sochi. And another World Cup title would be sweet."

"You're second in the standings, you've got a great shot," said my dad.

"Katya Hofstadter and I have been trading off top spot so far, but you never know, there are at least five other women barking at our heels."

"My money's on you." My dad gave me a proud once over.

"Well, anyway, doors will be wide open for you when you're ready to retire. There's still a lot of skiing you can do." My mom concentrated on putting her fork to her salad in a way that made me wonder if the salad had done wrong.

Things got quiet after that and I couldn't much stand the awkward silence. "Is there something going on?" A terrible thought occurred to me. "You're not sick, are you?"

"No. Of course not." My mother sounded vehement enough that I believed her but then she exchanged a look with my father and he sighed and bit his lip.

"We didn't want to say anything until after the holiday," she said.

"But?" I raised my eyebrows as dread crept down to my toes.

"Connor is getting married." She looked guilty, as though she'd been the one to arrange the marriage.

The news took my breath away. "Oh. Wow." It wasn't what I had expected and I felt a strange brew of emotions mucking around in my gut. Anger won out, anger fueled by betrayal and frustration, though what was missing was sadness and heartbreak. There was a part of me that was glad this was the news, my imagination had descended the depths to something so much worse.

No, my heart wasn't breaking and then I wondered what the hell was wrong with me that it wasn't. My parents were ready to be heartbroken on my behalf. "I'm so sorry, Mia," said my mom.

"Don't let it ruin your holiday. He was never good enough for you anyway." I took my dad's hand. I loved that he'd take my side, as though there were sides to be taken.

The holiday was hard to get through. News travels fast in a small town and by Christmas everyone knew about Connor and the new woman. They didn't say anything about it, of course. With me, they were extra cheerful, my Aunt Patty gave me a huge hug and told me how she'd heard about how well I'd done at Waterville. "You are amazing, just amazing," she gushed.

I was relieved when the day was over and although I loved my folks, I was relieved to get on a plane, glad to go to Europe and put an ocean between myself and Connor O'Keefe. Racing was my real life, the circuit was my life, and Connor would soon enough become just a blip in my past. That's what I told myself, anyway.

Nine

As much as I wanted to let my past with Connor go it nagged at me. How could he move on so quickly? Did he ever love me at all? Kept crossing through my brain all the way into Milan and up into Cortina.

It nagged at me so much I asked Rachel King, who was my roommate at the small resort hotel, as we unpacked our clothes. "Do you think I'm jealous? It's funny, I don't feel jealous."

"He's an asshole," said Rachel, putting her shirts into a drawer. This was exactly what I expected she would say, and I loved her for it.

"I could have married him, he asked me a couple of years ago."

I expected her to look surprised, but she kept sorting through her suitcase. "Maybe he isn't the guy for you." She looked up at me. "I think you ought to forget about him. Tell you what, when we finish with this meet and have handed those European girls their asses, we will go out on the town and find us some hot Italian dudes." She nodded as I shrugged. "Do not say no, Ice. You need to live a little. You are young, you are free, and you need to have some fun." She raised her eyebrows. "Be better than sorting socks in a lonely hotel room."

"Sorting socks? Jeez, I'm not that bad. I was planning a hot bath."

"Maybe we can find you someone to share the tub with."

I laughed. "Okay, I'm in."

The meet went well, though Katya managed to best me in both the combined and the giant slalom, which kept her in the top spot. Rachel won the downhill, which made her and the rest of us pretty happy and I came away with a win in the slalom.

"You can have first dibs on the shower," said Rachel as we gathered our gear at the end of the meet, "you're older, you need more time to get ready for a night out."

I went back to the hotel and pulled off my clothes and examined myself in the full length bathroom mirror. Freakishly tall for a women, and very muscular, I'd been called Amazonian and I'd never much minded it, but now I looked at myself as I figured a man would. I was a lot of things—strong, competitive, and maybe even imposing. What I wasn't was soft and curvy and small. I closed my eyes and told myself to cut it out. I'd had guys come on to me, it wasn't as if I was a pariah. Creech Crèches had been pretty interested once upon a time and, though I wasn't great at reading signals, I'd bet if I gave him a shove in that direction, I could hook him in still. Then I thought hook him? What is he, a fish? And then I thought what a bad idea hooking him would be in the first place.

I rarely evaluated myself like this and I told myself to quit it again as I blew dry my hair. Then I did something else I rarely did, I put on lipstick and mascara and a T-shirt that was tight and low enough to show cleavage. I might have been tall, but I had a good figure, I had long legs, I looked good in jeans. Or so I told my reflection in a mirror pep-talk.

"Wowza," said Rachel.

"Yeah, right," I said.

She cocked her head. "I've never known you to lack confidence, Ice. Don't disappoint me."

Reni joined us and we went to a noisy bar with a d-jay. Rachel was a flirt and she was soon dancing while Reni and I sipped drinks at a table crowded into the back of the room. Reni had gone home over the holiday and rekindled her budding relationship with Paul. I figured I'd sit all night and listen to her talk about finding true love. Maybe her happiness would rub off on me.

Then a tall dark-haired man asked me to dance and Reni stopped talking and nearly pushed me from the table. "Go, dance."

I did. We danced and he bought me a drink, though I was only half finished with the one I had set down in front of me. In broken English, he told me his name was Marco, that he was a car salesman from Milano and he was in Cortina for a ski holiday.

"And you is Mia Whitmeyer, I watch you ski slalom today. You ski marvelous."

"Thank you." Slalom wasn't my best event and a win in that event always made me especially proud. I took his compliment and stroked my ego with it. I told myself I had been bruised, badly, by Connor's news and I needed a few flattering words. I liked the way the guy was looking at me, too. Like I was a Ferrari he might not be able to afford, but he wanted anyway.

A slower number came on and he asked me to dance again. He held me close, he was a few inches taller than me and we were thigh to thigh. I closed my eyes and took in the scent of his cologne; something I imagined was expensive and Italian. Connor crossed my brain and I purposely chased the thought away. And then Creech inhabited my thoughts, dancing with me years ago, telling me he regretted not staying the night. I tried to chase the thought away, but he wasn't so easily displaced.

Marco stroked my back and he pulled me in even closer, close enough that I could feel his erection, kind of shocking and thrilling at the same time. "I think I like to leave now," he whispered, his voice gone gruff in my ear. "And I like you come leave too."

The drink I'd had, the music, the idea of someone wanting me, went to my head. "Okay."

Rachel and Reni exchanged looks when I went back to the table to get my jacket and announced I was leaving.

"Is that a good idea?" Reni asked. "You don't know him."

"That's the point," I turned to Rachel. "Don't wait up." She followed me toward the door, where Marco stood waiting. "Ice, I was kind of kidding about the bath thing." She looked pained.

"I'm a big girl, Rachel. I can take care of myself."

"Okay, just. Don't do anything stupid, okay?" The way she said it let me know she thought I'd already done a stupid thing.

Marco took my hand as we walked through Cortina village resort. It was a still and starry night and cold enough that our breath vaporized into clouds. Music and noise came from several clubs along the way.

"I stay at the pension, down this street." We turned down a quiet side alley, lit only by a street light. He stopped under the stain of the light and turned to me. "You are very beautiful, I think." He took a lock of my hair and ran it between his fingers. "Very beautiful." And then he pulled me in for a kiss. It was a deep kiss, his tongue angling into my mouth, his hand behind my head and his other hand coming to caress my shoulder and run down over my well covered breast.

I tried to get into it. I told myself I wanted this, I needed this; a romantic fling with a passionate young Italian man who smelled of expensive cologne and who would mean nothing in my life. I tried, but as I stood there and kissed him back for all I was worth, all I could think was it would be over soon and I'd feel worse for having done this. Then Creech waltzed back in to my brain and my next thought was that this guy's kisses weren't the ones I wanted.

I pulled back. "I'm sorry. This is a terrible idea."

He looked at me with questions in his eyes.

"I'm sorry," I repeated. "I can't." I turned and walked away, before he could say anything, hoping he didn't take it into his head to do something stupid or romantic like follow me and call my name.

He didn't follow and I turned the corner and he

was gone. I nearly ran back to our hotel, my heart hammering as my head asked what I had been thinking. I went into the lobby. A hot bath, alone, seemed like a good idea. A dark room and a bed to myself seemed an even better idea.

Creech stood at the bank of elevators, his back to me; we were the only people besides the concierge in the lobby. The elevator dinged, the door opened and he stepped inside. I ran to get into the car with him before the door shut. "Mia," he said, sounding surprised.

I grabbed his jacket and kissed him as though my life depended on it.

Creech

Her kiss came on me like a bullet leaving a gun; it found its target on my lips and in the center of my gut. Instinct took over, want took over. I had wanted Mia for a long, long time, and I kissed her back hard and put my arms around her and backed her up against the wall of the elevator car. The elevator pinged and the door opened and I reached back and groped around to try and shut it again.

She grabbed my hand. "Not here."

We stepped out of the elevator and I fished my room card from my pocket, telling myself not to think too hard. But my thoughts were racing. I stopped in front of my door to gather them. Mia took the key from me and unlocked the door.

I had a single room, small, with just enough room for a bed, a desk and chair, and a small dresser. You could barely walk around. Though I don't think walking was on either of our minds. She closed the door and I grabbed her shoulders. "Are you sure you want—"

She unzipped her jacket. "I don't want to think. Don't make me think."

I pulled off her jacket. I didn't want to think either. I kissed her. This was what I wanted. It was all I wanted.

Mia

I had walked into his room knowing if he stopped, if he gave me the regret speech again, I'd crumble up like used paper. No, I would stomp back out the door and bury myself in the darkness of my room.

He didn't give me the speech. He took my face between his hands and kissed me, the same way he'd kissed me in the elevator, hard and long and deep, and I knew it was exactly what I needed and what I wanted.

I pulled off my jacket, my lips still locked to his and we did this dance, he took off his jacket and then I let go for a minute and pulled off my shirt, thankful I'd thought to put on the one lacy bra I owned. He fingered the material whispered, "pretty," and kissed my neck and my shoulder and the space between my breasts. I put my face to his hair, he smelled of the outdoors, a scent so familiar it felt like coming home.

We took a few steps and fell onto the mattress, him on top of me. He raised himself up and pulled off his shirt and I ran my hand over his shoulders, muscular and well-defined, more powerful than my own. I took off my bra and the rest of my clothes followed, then his. And then he was on top of me, kissing my breasts, my belly, his hand caressing my thigh.

"Shit," he said and for a moment I had a sense of dread—not the regret thing, not now.

"Don't think."

He looked at me, his eyes telling me he wouldn't stop, maybe couldn't. "No condoms."

"My jacket pocket." Rachel had handed me two of them before going out. It was a kind of joke, but feeling wicked and wild; I stashed them in my pocket and laughed at myself for doing it. I wasn't the kind of girl who carried condoms in her jacket. Or I hadn't been, until now.

Creech raised his eyebrows. "Do I want to know?"
"Probably not."

I had never been with anyone but Connor and I remembered sex as being nice, a way to get close, but this—when Creech looked into my eyes there was a connection, as though there were a thin wire conducting electricity between us. I chased everything else from my head but that thin wire, and desire and instinct, and I was lost in the sensation; the hard muscles of his back under my hands, the weight of him pressing into me, his warm breath on my neck, and then his warm mouth on my skin, his tongue on my lips. I took him in, was greedy for him, and the world fell away as I fell.

Afterwards, he collapsed on top of me. "Mia," he kissed my shoulder and took my hand and kissed my fingers. "My amazing Mia." And my heart expanded as the beat of his pulse matched my own.

"Thank you," I whispered, feeling too emotional to say anything else.

He lifted his head and his eyes met mine. "You don't have to thank me for that. You'll never have to thank me for that."

Ten

I woke up as the morning light began pearling through the window, Creech's leg over mine, the warmth of his skin like an extra blanket against the cold. I closed my eyes for a moment more and breathed in the peace that enveloped the room, still drowsy and halfway in dreams. Then reality hit me like a bucket of cold water and I opened my eyes and the voice inside my head asked me what the hell I thought I was doing. I argued back that Creech and I were consenting adults; we could do as we pleased, but I knew the argument held no weight. He was my coach and sleeping with him was sleeping with the boss. It was a terrible idea. At best, it would cause a lot of friction with my teammates, something I didn't want and would break focus from my goal of capturing another World Cup title. At worst, it could get Creech fired. I was confident I wouldn't be thrown from the team, not as long as I kept winning anyway, but he was the new guy and there were at least four other guys who would be happy to take his job.

Stop it, I told myself, the assistant coaches didn't have it in for Creech, they liked him. We all liked him, but there was no denying that if he and I started something here, it would make his life difficult. Too late, though. We had started something and my heart didn't want to be put on hold. My head, though, my head told me I had to do what was right. Chalk it up to a mistake—Creech and I had let our libidos get the best of us. Lying there, with my head against his chest, the rise and fall of his breath under my ear, it sure didn't feel like a mistake. It hadn't been a mistake the night before either, I'd known exactly what I wanted and I had gotten it. Still, a relationship was a cost neither of us could afford.

    I glanced at the clock—five a.m. according to the glowing digits—and decided it would be best if I let Creech go. I managed to get out from under the tangle of his limbs—he was a solid sleeper and barely moved—and gathered the clothes scattered on the floor and got back into them. It felt illicit; I wasn't the kind of girl who snuck back to her room wearing yesterday's underwear after a one-night stand. At least, I hadn't been that girl until now. I put on my shoes and took one long last look back at the bed, fighting a compelling urge to climb back in and swallowing down some very bitter regret.

    "You are fantastic," I whispered, hoping maybe the words would hang in the air and reach into his dreams. "And I'm so, so sorry to leave like this." With that, I slipped out into the hall and shut the door with a gentle click.

    No one ever needs to know, I told myself as I stood there a moment longer. Then I looked up and saw Mary Tyco at the end of the hallway, staring at me. My heart dropped like a runaway elevator. So much for discretion. I took a deep breath and stared back with my best Ice race-day glower and then turned on my heel and walked towards my room.

    I wasn't sure if the stare fooled Mary. It sure hadn't fooled me and my brain was shooting around like a rocket. I didn't have to explain myself to a teenage rookie, I reasoned. Besides, she was half in love with Creech; anyone with eyes would have noticed the way she looked at him as though he were a movie star. If push came to shove, I'd appeal to her soft spot for him, and tell her rumor-mongering could kill his career.

    I slipped into my room, thinking I'd climb back into my own bed and pretend I'd come in late. If I knew Rachel at all, she would have danced until last call and fallen into a near stupor once her head hit the pillow. We were on our way to Garmisch, but the bus wouldn't leave until ten and more than once she'd gotten up fifteen minutes before departure, thrown on her clothes and run out the door with seconds to spare.

That morning, though, she came out of the bathroom as I came in. The minute she saw me, she pointed an accusatory finger at me. "Don't do that to me ever again."

"Do what?" I asked, feeling defensive.

"Don't hook up with some guy you don't even know and stay out all night. Did your mother never teach you about stranger danger?"

I would have laughed if she didn't look so serious. "As I recall, you were the one who insisted we go out."

"To dance, Ice. Not to have illicit sex with strangers." She looked me over again. "I hope you used protection."

I sat on the bed and grinned at her. Maybe I should have told her where I'd been, but it was easier to let her make assumptions. "I'm fine, as you can see for yourself. As I already told you, I'm a big grown up girl. I can make decisions for myself, thank you very much."

She sat down with a sigh. "Well, despite the wrinkled clothes, I guess there's no harm done. He was a hottie and lucky for you, turned out he wasn't a serial rapist."

"Nope. It's all good."

"So are you going to see him again?"

For a split second I forgot she was talking about Marco. Then I came to my senses. "No, I'm not going to see him again."

"Wowza, Ice. I would not have expected this of you. I hope the sex was good."

"Best I ever had." This made Rachel's eyes go wide, though she knew damn well I wasn't about to give her any details.

Creech

I wasn't surprised she was gone when I woke. I was angry, yes. And sad, too, at the thought she'd take this thing ignited between us and run from it.

Oh, I got why she did it. She knew our sleeping together wouldn't sit well with her teammates, or the other coaches for that matter. After the night we'd spent together, I didn't give a shit about any of that. And, when we'd made love, she hadn't given a shit about it either. It had been terrific. Better than terrific.

I went into the bathroom and, since I hadn't bothered to throw on any clothes, jumped into the shower. I turned the water up hot as I could and then switched it to cold. The spray stabbed me, blades of ice against my skin, and I wasn't sure what I was trying to do. If I had to put a name to it, I guess I'd say I was trying to freeze her out, out of my chest, out of my groin, out of my heart. Because, in leaving, she made it clear she had no interest in returning and the thought of never being with her again, of last night being a one-off, was sharp enough to shred me.

I was falling for her. No, not falling, that implied I hadn't already hit bottom. I had fallen and as I stood there, the water numbing my skin, I knew I'd done the one thing I promised myself I'd never do again. I was in love with a woman who wasn't ready to love me back. Unrequited love, the bitch, refused to leave me alone.

I got out, dried off and looked at my reflection—tired eyes, I needed a shave. "You really know how to pick 'em, buddy," I told myself. Last thing I needed was another friendship with a woman I loved. The first one had nearly done me in. I had, finally, made peace with the notion that Mallory Prescott and I would never be more than friends. I was finally good with it and then Mia came along.

I was tempted to call Mallory and tell her I'd done it again. It was no good to dredge up the past, but there I was, back in high school, giving my heart to Mallory, who managed to hand it back to me. Back then, in the way of teenage boys, I'd figured Mallory would always be there for me. I was so focused on being a world class racer that I put her on the sidelines, and figured if I looked up, she'd be standing there, cheering me on.

When I got called up to the U.S. team, it felt like I'd been handed the world with a big blue ribbon tied around it. I'd worked so hard to get the nod, and I'd gotten it. My head was bigger than a helium balloon. I was about to have it all—my racing career and a hot girlfriend who loved me.

I left for training camp a month after high school graduation. In the time between, I decided I wanted to cement my relationship with Mallory. I figured I owed her as much. I went and bought a tiny chip of a diamond. A few days before I was set to leave, Mallo and I climbed out to our favorite make-out spot, a promontory on the backside of Ridge Run, the ski area our parents co-owned. I put the diamond in the pocket of my khakis and was nervous as hell on the twenty-minute climb. I fell to one knee as soon as we reached our destination, confusing Mallory, who actually asked "What are you doing?" though I'd guess by the time she got the words out of her mouth, she'd figured it out.

"Isn't it obvious? I'm proposing." I fished the ring from my pocket and held it out.

I don't know what I expected; Mallory wasn't the kind of girl who jumped up and down squealing. I didn't expect what happened—she knelt down beside me and, with tears in her eyes, said, "Creech, we can't do this." She closed my fist around the ring.

I got mad, so mad I couldn't think straight. I got up off my knee. "What the hell do you mean, we can't?"

"I mean we can't get married. Not right now."

"You said you loved me. You told me you loved me like a million times. Dammit Mallory, this is what people in love do. "

She was all out crying now, still on her knees. "We can't."

I should have let her explain, but if I'd stood there a minute more I would have been crying myself and I couldn't let myself be that vulnerable, not after she'd hurt me like she just had. I walked away and made my way back down the trail as fast as I could. She didn't try to follow.

Years and distance had given me a different perspective. Mallory was right, we were barely eighteen and neither of us was ready to get married. She'd watched her parents fight their way out of a bad marriage and, when they finally divorced, she'd been not angry but relieved it was finally over. But, back then, I was so hurt I wasn't going to speak to her ever again.

She showed up while I was packing. My mom brought her up to my room and I couldn't very well slam the door on the two of them, so I let Mallory in and she sat on the bed. "I'm really proud of you," she said.

My dad had said the same thing, and while I was glad to hear it from him, it wasn't nearly as welcome coming from the girl I was in love with. I scoffed at the comment and turned my back on her, and stuffed socks in between the neatly folded shirts in my suitcase.

She wasn't so easily put off. "It's not that I don't love you. I do."

"But you don't love me enough to marry me."

"I love you too much." I turned to see her looking at me, her eyes bright with hurt. "You are destined to do great things, you're about to start a whole new life. I'd just get in the way."

I wanted to tell her it wasn't true, but a voice deep inside told me she was right. It hurt like hell, but I knew something else, too. She wasn't about to change her mind.

Years passed and, much as I didn't want to, I still loved Mallory. A small part of me hoped she'd come around; she'd change her mind. And then she met Bell and I knew; she loved him in a way she'd never loved me. I could tell just by the way she looked at him, they were so right together. So I swallowed down my feelings and resolved never to let what happened with Mallory happen again.

And now I'd fallen for Mia, who had walked out on me. Though, I would have sworn on my life—given the way she'd looked at me last night, the way she'd made love, she'd fallen for me, too.

Mia

I spent a lot of time on buses winding their way through narrow alpine passes in my ten years on the team. We usually passed the time listening to music, or reading, or chatting. Sometimes we played cards. Tinny used to trounce me at poker with fair regularity—we would bet crazy and I think I still owe her an island in the Pacific and a vintage Rolls Royce. Thinking about Tin made me miss her right down to my toes. She was the only one I could have confided in about this thing with Creech.

I thought about calling her, and maybe I would once we got settled in our hotel, though privacy was at a premium. Then, thinking again, I decided no—it wasn't something I wanted to discuss over the phone and, besides, she had her own deal with the baby coming, I didn't need to burden her with mine.

The ride from Cortina to Garmisch was a long one and, on that day, it seemed a nearly endless series of winding turns and narrow passes. The scenery was beautiful—Alpine peaks covered in snow, pines with low lying branches decked in white, all glistening in the sun under a clear blue sky. I closed my eyes and tried to sleep, ear buds in my ears though I wasn't listening to anything. Rachel, in the seat next to mine, thought I'd spent the night having illicit sex with a stranger and that I might be hung over to boot, so she took pity and pretty much left me alone.

Creech was somewhere in the back with a couple of the assistant coaches. I'd gotten on before him, wanting to avoid him and still I managed to inadvertently catch his eye as he climbed aboard, a look full of hurt he quickly covered as he moved to his seat. Mary, too, caught my eye, her eyes narrowed when we exchanged glances and then she, too, looked away.

The ride went on and on, my thoughts turning

over the night. I wanted to make amends. I wanted to be with Creech, but we can't always get what we want. I ruminated and ruminated and by the time the bus crossed the border into Germany, I felt I'd been on it for most of my life.

Maybe it was my feelings, a mixed up cocktail of lust and anger at the unfairness of it all, thinking I can't get involved with Creech, and then thinking to hell with it, let everyone believe what they're going to believe, that got in the way of my performance at Garmisch. Then again, maybe I was making excuses. In the past, I'd funneled all those emotions into my passion for facing down the hill, for skiing hard and fast and pulling out all the stops to win. Bottom line was, I finished twentieth in the downhill, which for me was downright lousy. It messed with my standing—Katya skied to a fourth place, enough to keep her at the top of the standings and widen the narrow margin between us. Monika Stueben, the German phenom who was also the local girl, won the race in a big way, enough to push her into second and run me down the ladder a notch. Five other girls were chomping on my heels, including Rachel, who finished second.

Though there were four more events in the meet, I knew I'd have to get my head together if I wanted things to improve. I went back to the warmup hut and sat with my head in my hands. It was only one race. But it was a big race and it would be tough to redeem myself in the next downhill, in Innsbruck, which was Katya's hometown. She always skied big for the home crowd.

Reni came in and sat down next to me and began pulling off her boots. She gave me a look that said it all, and so before she could open her mouth to console me, I said "I know, it's just one race." I smiled at her, though I didn't feel much like smiling.

"Hell, I'm honored to have bested you." She'd come in twelfth, good for her as downhill wasn't her specialty.

"You've bested me before, Reni. You are a hell of a skier." I meant it, she was.

"Thanks, Ice. But when you're on, nobody can catch you. Not even Katya."

I sighed. "On being the operative word. I wasn't there, Reni. My head wasn't in it."

She nodded. "Rachel told me. About the Italian guy."

"Rachel has a big mouth." Honestly, I couldn't figure out if I was mad at Rachel or just amused at the whole thing. The girl couldn't keep a secret if her life depended on it.

"You can tell me it's none of my business, but I think you ought to call him."

"Why would I do that?"

"You said yourself your head wasn't in the race today. Well, have you ever considered it might be because you've fallen in love?" She held up a hand. "Before you tell me I'm wrong, think about it. It can happen fast, I know that's how it was with Paul. One look, and I just knew."

"I'm not in love with Italian Marco. I have some stuff to straighten out in my head, but he's not one of them."

"You're sure about that?"

"Yes, I'm sure." I don't know if she was convinced, because she was right. I had fallen in love with the guy I'd spent the night with.

Creech

Mia avoided me as though I had bubonic plague, talking to me in single words only when necessary. She had a bad finish, for her anyway, in the downhill and I knew it must have upset her, but she was a champion for a reason. The next day she came back and owned the downhill in the combined, and then she roared in

Super G, her best event overall. She beat out the field by so much that, despite a slow slalom where she' nearly missed a gate, it put her in second place, within a hair's width of Katya's narrow lead.

Mary Tyco came up to talk to me after the slalom. She'd done well, placing in the top fifteen, which was good for a newbie, though I also knew she wanted to be on top and wouldn't like settling for that placement. I figured that was what she wanted to talk to me about, which would have been a simple talk. I'd tell her she'd done fine. I'd remind her she was competitive and she worked hard and if she kept at it she'd be on top eventually. I was ready to give her this speech when she asked, "Are you sleeping with Mia Whitmeyer?" which knocked me totally off my path and left me tongue tied for a minute.

It also put me on the defensive. "Why would you ask me that?"

"Because I saw her leaving your room at like five o'clock in the morning."

Maybe I should have told her the truth. I wanted to, but a lie came spinning out of my mouth. "She forgot her key."

Mary narrowed her eyes as though she didn't believe me. It was a lame explanation, but then, maybe because she wanted to believe it, she said, "Okay. Sorry I asked."

We had some down time in Garmisch, the slalom had finished out in the morning and the bus to Innsbruck, our next stop on the circuit, wouldn't leave until noon the following day. We all, coaches and skiers, usually took these small respites to relax—racing can be grueling and so there were trips into the little town, or time spent just sitting with a book or some music. I wanted to spend the time with Mia, though I knew it might not be wise, especially now that Mary's radar had been alerted. Still, I felt I at least needed to talk to her, if only to clear the air between us.

I found her on the outside patio of a café next to the hotel, where she sat by herself, sipping a coffee and seemingly lost in thought as she stared out at the mountains that rose steeply behind the busy thoroughfare. I bought a coffee and asked if I could join her, which seemed to startle her.

"Sure." She nodded towards the seat across from her.

I studied the cup, not sure how to move forward. There was so much I wanted to say and none of it seemed like enough. "Mary told me she saw you leave my room."

Mia sighed and closed her eyes. "That little shit," she said under her breath. "What did you tell her?"

"You lost your room key."

Mia scoffed at this. "And she believed you?"

"I don't know. She seemed to. I think she wants to believe me." I let my eyes catch hers, pretty blue, the color of the winter sky. "I wanted to tell her the truth"

"You didn't though." She looked out at towards the mountains again. "Because you don't want to lose your job over a fling."

She might as well have slapped me. "I think it's a little more than a fling, or I am really bad at reading things?"

"It can't be more, Creech. You know that." Why was it I always fell for hard-headed stubborn women?

"I don't know that, Mia. Maybe I do want more, have you even ever considered how I feel ? Or do my feelings not enter the equation at all?"

"Why do you think I'm..." She looked at me again, her eyes filling, then she blinked and shook her head and stood up. "I can't be responsible for you losing your job. And that could happen. I can't be responsible for the conflict it would cause. So yeah, I have considered it. I have considered it over and over and, no matter how I try to make it otherwise, I always come up with the same answer. We can't." Then she walked off and it took all the resolve in my body not to go after her.

Mia

I threw myself into preparing for the next race. I needed a downhill win, a decisive one, to clear the top position in the standings again. Innsbruck would be a hard-fought competition—as I've mentioned, it was Katya's hometown and she always did exceptionally well with the hometown crowd cheering her on.

The hill conditions were just the way I liked them, hard and icy, which made for faster times, though it was easier to lose control. I had a really good training run and, on the day of the race, I was ready to devour the course.

Innsbruck was bitterly cold, a strong wind came up through the mountains and brought with it wind chills well below zero. It swept the snow from the course and left it glistening, the jumps sharp and unforgiving.

I pulled a fifth place start, right behind Katya, and as I waited my turn, I jumped up and down a few times to keep the sharp wind from stiffening my limbs. I blew into my hands before putting on my gloves to keep my fingers from freezing.

Then I was in the gate. "She was fast," said Creech, referring to Katya's run, the results of which had just been radioed up. "You're faster. You own this thing. Now go."

I nodded and listened to the countdown and the start beep, the wand against my shin gave way and I let loose. The first part of the course was steep and I rode the grade, gaining speed as I descended. My skis chattered over the ice and still I accelerated. I threw myself into the turn, my edge carving into the hill, at the boundary of control, right where I wanted to be. The first jump was ahead, I got into position and was airborne in an instant, my body a missile projecting forward, I hit the ice again, without losing much velocity and went into the flats. Another turn, another steep and I knew, I knew I had it. If I could hang onto the pace, if I could hold the speed, one more jump, a short steep to the finish and no one would beat my time.

It happened so fast I didn't register it at first. My skis chattered around the turn, my right edge caught and in a split second, my ski was out from under me. If I hadn't been all out, if I'd been a little slower, if my weight hadn't been shifted far to one side to make the turn, I would have gotten it under control and pulled the ski back. I'd done it before. But I was fast and the ice was unforgiving and the turn was on the steep and when my ski flew out from under me, gravity and velocity became the enemy and in another split second I knew I had lost the battle. I fell hard, so hard it made my teeth chatter. A deep pain undulated in my hip. It radiated upward as I saw the orange snow fence, the netting around the trail, race towards me. And then the world went black.

Part Two
After

Eleven

Creech

The world is full of *if only*; if only it hadn't been so icy, if only the wind chill hadn't been so bad, if only she hadn't been blazing down the course at breakneck speed. It didn't do any good to think about these things, but they kept on, in an endless film loop, as I skied down to where she lay crumpled in the netting. It continued as I stood there, the wind numbing my limbs, as the EMTs worked on her and strapped her to a backboard. It didn't stop even after the EVAC helicopter added an extra gust that tore at the trees before carrying her away.

They took her to the University of Innsbruck hospital. The orthopedic spinal center there was one of the finest in the world and that was some consolation at least. I called Mike Greenburg and told him what had happened. And then I went back to the base lodge to make a call to Mia's parents.

I found her parents' number on an emergency contact list in the computer, took a couple of deep breaths, and dialed my cell phone. A woman answered the phone. "Mrs. Whitmeyer? It's Joel Crèches, Mia's coach?"

"Yes?" Already the voice sounded braced for impact. Why else would I be calling?

I kept my voice steady as I told her what had happened; my hand shook as badly as an alcoholic who needed a drink.

Mia's mother was surprising calm. Maybe the full force of what I'd said hadn't hit her yet. Maybe she was in shock. "University Hospital, you said?"

"Yes. Innsbruck."

"We'll be there soon as we can." There was a pause. "Mr. Crèches? Could you be there when she wakes up? I hate for her to think she's all alone."

"Sure, yes. Of course." I hadn't thought about much, not beyond what came next, and now I knew the hospital was the only place I could be. I called Davey on the hill.

"They're ready to start up again in twenty minutes," he told me.

"Yeah, I need you to take over. I'm going to stay with Mia." It wasn't my job to sit around waiting for news; my job was to be on the hill with the team.

I waited for an argument from Davey, but after a moment's pause, he said, "Okay, do what you need to do."

The hospital was clean and white, sterile, and dismal as hell. I was assaulted by reporters from the German and Austrian media in the lobby. By tonight, Mia's accident would be all over the news.

Mia was in surgery, and no one could tell me when she'd be out. I got an assurance that the surgeon would come and talk to me when it was over and more than that I didn't and couldn't know. I went to the cafeteria, where they allowed cell phones and bought myself a cup of coffee. It reminded me of Garmisch, Mia sitting there with tears in her eyes telling me we couldn't pursue a relationship. I should have taken her into my arms, I should have told her I loved her and nothing, no job, no race, no World Cup title could measure against that. Now, maybe it was too late.

She was young and she was stronger than most women. If anyone could pull through, it was Mia. I tried to cling to that thought, the only positive thing in my head, but it kept getting displaced by the terrible emptiness I was feeling. For the first time since I'd taken the coaching job, I felt far from home, lost, and as though I belonged nowhere and to no one.

I didn't particularly like hospitals, though I'd guess not too many people counted them among their favorite places. I'd spent too much time in them—after my accident, and last year, when Mallory's little girl, Emily, had fallen from a tree and been rushed to the ICU at Fletcher Allen in Burlington, Vermont, a hospital miles from home. Bell had been away when Emily had her accident and I'd spent a few days at the hospital with Mallory. I had done it as a friend and I understood how terrible the experience was for Mallory. But I hadn't, until now, fully felt what she must have gone through, how coming so close to losing someone you care so deeply about could bring you close to losing yourself.

I took my cell phone from my pocket and turned it over in my hand. I hadn't talked to Mallory since I'd seen her briefly over the Christmas break. I'd promised to call regularly when I'd left for Park City and I hadn't done it. It pained me to think we'd grown distant; it pained me more to know how much I needed her just now.

I called anyway. She answered on the fourth ring, her voice groggy. "Creech?"

"Yeah. I haven't called in a while and—" My throat closed and the room began swimming away.

"Creech, are you okay?"

I nearly said I was fine, but what would be the point? "It's Mia," my voice broke.

"Mia Whitmeyer?"

When I could talk I said, "She's had an accident. They air-evaced her to the hospital."

"Oh, Creechie. That's terrible. Where are you?"

"In the hospital. In Innsbruck. Waiting for news. She's in surgery." I stopped short of saying she might not make it out and I can't lose her. I couldn't give voice and life to that fear.

A man's voice came up in the background. Bell's voice, asking who was calling at this hour. I did the math; it was four o'clock in the morning in Lake Placid. "Oh, God, I'm sorry. I forgot the time difference."

"Don't worry about it. Look, if there's anything we can do, you've got it."

There was nothing, though, was there? Nothing she or anyone could do. "No, I just, I needed to hear a familiar voice. Go on back to sleep okay?"

"You take care of yourself, promise?"

"Sure. I promise." I hung up feeling even emptier than I had before I'd called.

Mia

Maybe it was the drugs they gave me, but I had the most magical dreams. I couldn't remember them all, except for this one—I am sitting on a couch in front of a fieldstone fireplace. It's like my place in Park City, but not quite. It's snowing and the fire is roaring, it's warm and bright. My head is on Creech's shoulder and then I close my eyes and his lips are on mine, firm and warm and so full of love I think my heart will explode. My eyes open, in the dream I want to see his face, and this is where I woke up, a white ceiling overhead, a monitor beeping near my ear, pain rising like a tide, my chest in the grip of it. "Ow." I'm not sure I said this out loud. No one seemed to hear.

I raised my hand to look at it, an IV stuck in between my fingers. And then Creech was there and I thought maybe this was just the next part of the dream.

"You're here."

He looked so tired, unshaved, like he hadn't slept or showered in a while. "You're awake."

I wasn't sure I was awake, though something was wrong and I needed to tell him. "I love you," I said. He pushed the hair off my forehead, his fingers warm. "I love you," I said again, in case he hadn't heard. And I drifted back to sleep.

Creech

"I love you, too," I said, though I was pretty sure she couldn't hear me. She was on some heavy duty drugs and her eyes were glazed over when she said it to me, if she was talking to me. I wasn't sure if she'd even seen me, or if she'd mistaken me for someone else.

Still, she'd been awake, and that was a good thing and the rock sitting on my chest rolled away. I had just spent the worst twenty-four hours of my life at her bedside, worse even than the time after my own accident. Or maybe, it was a question of distance—it had been over ten years since what happened in Grindlewald. Although, as I sat there, with nothing to do but watch Austrian TV or stare at the white walls, it all came back to me in all its gory glory, another film loop I couldn't make disappear. There I was again, looking over the steep in the start house, the beeping count, the coach cheering, "Go, go, go" and I'm skating over the start of the downhill run. It was a training run and the coach's instruction had been to keep it reigned in. The idea was to learn the course, then come back for the race the next day and explode out of the gate and ski like you were on fire.

I was still young enough, then, to believe in my immortality and I didn't want to do anything in a small way, so when I came from the start in the training run I went for it, my skis blowing through the hard pack as I gained speed. I loved that speed, the feeling of going fast, of being on the edge of possible. Sometimes you ski too close to those edges and you fall over them, you tumble hard and fast. I learned that in Grindlewald. One moment I was unstoppable and the next the air I'd taken on the jump grew turbulent, gravity pulled me down and then over and the next I was caught in the nets, blinking up at the sky.

I had hit the air at eighty miles an hour, I knew because the coaches, then and now, climb the pines lining the course with speed guns. Mia, before she hit the fences, had been trucking out at close to ninety. In the split second over the edge, I had torn the cartilage in both my knees, displaced my hip and broken my femur. Mia had bested me there, too. She'd broken both femurs and her pelvis. She had a minor concussion and, thought the surgeon was optimistic, he did mention there was a possibility of nerve damage. Possibility of nerve damage, I'd been around racing long enough to know what it meant— if she'd messed up her spine, she was unlikely to walk, let alone ski, again.

The uncanny similarity of our falls wasn't lost on me and I wondered if there wasn't a demonic force in the universe, rubbing its hands together and cackling. Still, she was alive. She had survived and she would survive. It was going to be okay, I told her and myself as I stood there, her limp hand in mine. I brought her hand to my face and ran the back of it over my cheek. "It'll be okay, you'll see," I repeated.

Her parents walked into the room then, looking about as tired as I felt. Mia had inherited her bright blue eyes from her father, his eyes set on me now with questions in them. I let go of his daughter's hand.

"She was awake, for a few minutes. They said she'd be in and out, they have her on painkillers."

Her mom, blonde and surprisingly small given Mia's stature, went to stand across the bed from me and ran her hand over the sheet. "Thank you, Mr. Crèches, for staying with her."

"It's Creech. I didn't want her to be here alone."

"That was kind of you." Mia's father stood beside

his wife, the two of them looking down at Mia as though she were a baby in a cradle. Her mom straightened back Mia's hair.

"Have you talked to the surgeon?" I asked.

Her dad looked up. "He said she'd need to stay here for at least a month. He talked about a second surgery."

"Our team orthopedic is flying in to look at her. The team, all of us, would do anything for Mia."

They both looked at me now and I wondered if they thought we, the team, skiing, had already done enough. If she hadn't been a racer, she wouldn't be lying here now.

"How did it happen?" her mom asked.

"It was a fluke, she looked great, and she was fast, really fast. Her ski came out from under her and that was it." I didn't know how else to explain, how a split second had changed their daughter's life. But then, they knew the risks she took. They'd seen her race hundreds of times.

"She was unconscious," I continued, "but it was a minor concussion. She fell on her hip." I told myself to stop talking. "I'm going to go, talk to the team, give you some time with her," I said. And I left before the culpability I felt in Mia's accident did me in.

Mia

I woke up again, this time my parents were both staring down at me. "Hey, sweetie," said my dad. I wasn't sure if I was awake or not, still in a haze, though there was a terrible throbbing in my chest, like someone was trying to stab their way out of it. The pain and look in their eyes told the story, I was awake and it was bad.

"We still in Austria?"

"Yes, baby," said my mom. "We were on the first plane here."

It was really bad. I wanted to go back to my dreams. "Where's Creech?' I asked.

"He's with the team," said my dad. I wondered if I'd dreamed him up before. It was entirely possible I'd been hallucinating.

The accident came back to me. I could see the fence rush toward me, the jarring in my hip, though there wasn't any pain, just numbness, and then it all disappeared. And now, here I was, in a hospital bed. "I really messed me up, didn't I?"

My mom tried to smile away the sadness in her eyes, but it was there, plain as the white wall of the room. "You're here. That's all that matters."

Her words confused me. Here was a hospital room. It didn't seem like such a great version of here. Better to be in a hotel room joking around with Rachel and Reni. Then it occurred to me, what she was telling me. Here was better than nowhere. They'd been worried I wouldn't make it through. I tried to sit up and that's when the second part of this disaster hit me. I couldn't.

My dad noticed the struggle. "You need to lie still, sweetie."

I put my head back on the pillow and stared at my feet, tented out under the blanket. I tried to wiggle my toes. I couldn't.

Twelve

Creech

The Innsbruck meet went on without me or Mia; the combined had been run with an easy win for Katya Hofstadter and the racers and coaches were gearing up for three more events before the short hop over to Kitzbuhel, next stop on the tour. Davy Delacroix met me in the hotel lobby. "The press is all over the place. Mike called; he thinks we ought to do a press conference."

The last thing I wanted was to get up in front of a bunch of sports reporters and talk about Mia, but it was my job. In some small way, I could do her justice this way; I could quell any rumors that might be floating around. "Okay, can you give me an hour? I need a shower. And I'd like to talk to the girls first. Can you call a team meeting?"

I went to my room, took off the clothes I'd slept in and lay down on the bed. An image of Mia's dad kept floating into my brain, the way he'd swallowed deep when I'd asked him about the surgeon, like he wanted to gulp down his fear and his worry. That line of thinking wasn't helping so I got up and got into the shower and let the water pour down over my head. Was it only a few days ago I'd been feeling put out because Mia had left my bed without waking me up? That whole incident seemed so incredibly small in comparison. All I wanted was to go back to the hospital, to sit with her. All I wanted was to never leave her.

I put on a fresh shirt and a pair of khakis; at least I could look like I was put together for the meeting, even if I didn't feel the part. The hotel had a small conference room, big enough for five rows of chairs, five wide on each aisle. They'd set up a podium in the front of the room and a big poster with an FIS ski logo covered the back wall for the cameras.

I'd asked Davey to gather the team and the coaches first—all in all there were about twenty-five of us, enough to fill half the room. I was surprised to see the place filled to overflow. There were racers from all over the world and quite a few of their coaches as well. They all turned as I walked in, the concern etched on their faces making my emotional state less steady. I took a deep breath.

In the front row were the rest of my team and next to Rachel and Reni sat Katya Hofstadter with her husband, Hans Jorgen, her hand tight in his. I nodded to them as I got up behind the podium and Davey shut the door. I took another deep breath and decided the podium was ridiculous. These were people I knew, they were here out of concern for Mia. The last thing they needed was me being distant and formal.

Up close and personal, though, that was rough. I came to the front of the room and all eyes were on me. I cleared my throat. "Mia's awake, I spoke with her briefly. She came through surgery great. Her parents are with her now." I watched Katya's hand twist tighter into Hans Jorgen's, then looked at Rachel, which was a mistake, because her eyes were filled and she was biting her lip. Something broke inside and I glanced away again to regain myself. I should have, maybe, told them all she was going to be fine. But the truth was I didn't know she was going to be fine and I didn't want to lie to them.

"She's um, the first few hours were touch and go, but she's stable. She's going to be in the hospital for a while. Beyond that, I really don't know." I probably should have added a pep talk, that's what they would have done in the movies, isn't it? I would have challenged them to ski well, to do it for Mia, to win for Mia. My heart weighed a thousand pounds in my chest. A win wouldn't get Mia out of the hospital any faster, any better.

Mia

I was out of my body looking down, fascinated, at the toes that wouldn't move on command. This was probably due to the drugs. I felt woozy and the nurse came in to explain the morphine drip, how I could push the button when I needed relief.

All my life, my body had responded to my brain like a well-oiled machine. It was something I took for granted, like breathing, though plenty of people had written and remarked on my split-second timing, my quick reflexes, and my strength. I'd build an entire career on those things and now my toes had up and called it quits. I wanted to yell at them for their insolence and insubordination, as though they were somehow not still a part of me.

My mom filled the room with cheerful chatter, talking about going to rehab in Hanover, near home, when I was ready, about how she'd called Tin and Aunt Patty and my brother Sebastian and how there were no doubt messages from all three of them in my phone. I usually loved how she could cheer a room, she was good at it, but right now I was tuning her out, too busy trying to make my toes dance.

"Damn it." I said.

"What's wrong?" asked my dad, who had sat quietly listening to my mom.

Everything was wrong, I wanted to tell them. I might have, had my dad not come back to my bedside looking like I'd just suggested the earth had stopped rotating on its axis. I wet my lips and said, "Thirsty." My mom hastened to pour me a cup of ice water from the tray at the side of the bed.

As she poured, a man in a lab coat walked into the room. He had white blond hair, and ice blue eyes, coloring so light he could have been an albino. My mom stopped what she was doing and put down the pitcher. My dad stood up again. The man nodded to both of them and came over to me. "I am Doctor Schuler," he said in a thick German accent. "I am doing the surgery on you, yes?"

I examined his hands, long fingers wound around the side-bar of my bed. He didn't look that much older than me, which didn't inspire confidence. "I talk earlier to your mother and your father and now I come to speak with you." His voice was formal, far away. I knew he had probably saved my life, but I wished he would act like a human rather than an automaton.

"I can't move my toes," I said. I knew there was a challenge in my voice. I wanted to tell him, in a few words, that he'd fucked up and he needed to fix it.

"Yes, this is no doubt so. You have had a spinal shock."

Spinal shock sounded like something out of a horror movie. I winced and my dad, standing now at the other side of the bed, took my hand. The doctor's face softened. "It is trauma to the spine," he explained as though I couldn't have figured that out for myself.

I took a deep breath. I didn't want to ask it, and particularly not of this arrogant prick who had left me lying here and just said, oh by the way, you have a spinal shock and that's why you can't move your damn toes. "So does this mean I'm paralyzed?" I hated that I couldn't keep the tremor from my voice. I bit the inside of my cheek; at least I still had some feeling there.

A big part of me hoped he'd say, "No, of course not. Silly girl, it's just the drugs we're giving you." He looked at his hands. "Yes. We are giving you the steroids; they will help with the swelling. And you are in the traction; we must keep you very still to stabilize the spine."

I closed my eyes, wanting to be anywhere but here. "It will take time, Ms. Whitmeyer," he said quietly. "We must wait and see how bad is the damage."

"How bad is the damage," I repeated. "What does that mean?"

"If it is well, the paralysis will slowly go away."

"And if it is not well?" I had opened my eyes to stare at him. My best Ice stare, though I wasn't managing it.

"Then the paralysis will stay."

Creech

The press conference was easier. I told them the same thing I told the racers and coaches; she was out of danger, but her prognosis was unknown. They asked the usual questions about what it meant to the team and I gave them the platitudes they expected; it would be tough, she would be missed, the girls were ready to try and fill the gap. I wanted to shout at them and tell them they could answer their own stupid questions. Of course, there was a hole in the team. It was nothing, though, compared to the hole in my heart.

I went back up to my room and lay down. I closed my eyes but there was no way I could shut off the thoughts rolling through my head. I got up, grabbed my keys and wallet, and headed for the door. The hospital was only twenty minutes away, and I had rented a car for three days.

Rachel and Reni were coming into the lobby as I was leaving it. "Hey, Coach," said Reni. "You have a rental car, right? Could Rachel and I borrow it tomorrow evening? We want to go see Ice, if that's okay."

"Yeah, sure, okay. Yeah. Tomorrow." I walked away without telling them where I was going. I was too unsure of myself to say anything.

I stopped at the hospital gift shop; not wanting to go to her room empty handed, and agonized over the choices. None of the gifts seemed anywhere close to right. It was getting late, and so I grabbed a teddy bear in a T-shirt, with a heart on the shirt. It didn't begin to express all I wanted to say, but I bought it anyway and tucked it under my arm.

The door to her room was open, just one dim light on inside. She was alone, head turned away from the door, staring out the window. The daytime view, I remembered, was one a lot of folks would have paid good money for; a postcard perfect look at the Tyrolean Alps that circled Innsbruck. But in the dark, all you could see was a reflection; the foot of the bed and the door. She must have seen my reflection, because she turned to me, her face solemn.

I held out the bear. "I had to leave in a hurry this afternoon. You were still kind of out of it and well, I wanted to see you."

She took the bear and traced her finger over his ear. "Okay, you've seen me. I'm awake. Tada." She studied the bear's face, her eyes so sad that I wanted to climb into the bed with her and hold her.

"Your parents here?"

"I told them to go to a hotel. I'm tired. They're tired."

She continued holding the bear, not looking at me again. I poked through my head for something to fill the silence. "Dr. Reynolds should be here tomorrow," I said of the team orthopedist I'd never met.

"Yes. I know. I hope he has a better bedside manner than the asshole that operated on me."

I could have defended the guy. He may well have saved her life, but it didn't seem the right thing to do just then. "Rachel and Reni want to come by and visit tomorrow evening."

"They don't have to. Better they keep their minds on racing. It's a long season."

"Yeah, look, about that. I could drive down from Kitzbuhel. It's only an hour from here." The idea occurred to me just then and I was already thinking how I could hang on to the rental for another week.

Mia pulled the teddy's arm. "You going to drive in from Norway, too?" There was a hard edge to her voice.

It was true, after next week, we'd be in Norway and then Sweden, and you couldn't easily drive to Innsbruck from there. Though I swear I would have tried it if possible. "I want to be here for you, that's all."

"Well, you can't be here, can you? This is where it all comes apart again. Our timing still sucks."

"It does suck, but it's not impossible." I stroked the back of teddy's head with my finger. "I've been where you are, Mia. I promise you, this is the worst part."

She let go of the bear and examined the IV stuck to the back of her hand. "Is it? You're not me. You walked out of the hospital. I can't move my damn toes, so I'm not walking anywhere. So, please, take your teddy bear and sympathy and go back to your job. I'm not part of it anymore."

Mia

I saw the terrible hurt in his eyes. I put it there and I knew I'd done it. I wanted him to hurt the way I hurt. I couldn't have said why, I never thought myself a vindictive person. Maybe it was because I'd fallen for him, or maybe because I'd lain there for hours trying to get my feet to move, trying to close my eyes and hoping sleep would take me. When I dreamed, I dreamed of him and maybe that was it, I wanted him to understand.

He took me at my word. "Keep the bear," he said. Then he touched my hand for a minute and walked out.

I closed my eyes and pressed the morphine button. Then I took the bear and hugged him tightly. I decided I'd call him Joel, not that many people knew Creech's given name and it would be my private connection to him. I felt a like a five-year-old, lying there with my teddy and hoping sleep would come and that, if it did, it would take me back to the dream I'd had of Creech and the warm fire, the cold world left outside.

Thirteen

Dr. Reynolds, the orthopedist from Salt Lake, came in the morning with Dr. Schuler. It was before visiting hours, so I was by myself, a half-eaten roll and a decapitated soft boiled egg in an egg cup still on my breakfast tray. The two of them looked down at me as though I were a puzzle they needed to solve. I can't say I liked it much, though Dr. Reynolds was an older guy, more my dad's age than mine, which made me feel better. I pushed the tray aside and then, as a second thought, put Joel on it, feeling ridiculous for having a stuffed animal in my bed.

"I've read through your chart," Dr. Reynolds began. "And had a long conversation with Dr. Schuler." He nodded to the younger doctor. "You are very fortunate to have this guy on your team, Mia. He's one of the best in the world."

I looked at my toes so I wouldn't roll my eyes. Enough with the mutual admiration society. "He's explained, about the spinal shock?" Dr. Reynolds asked.

"Yes. He's told me."

"Good, good. We'll see how you do with the steroids and traction, which will aid in healing. I can't stress how important it is for you to stay still for the next few weeks. I know that's not something you're used to doing." He chuckled as though I were a little kid who got into trouble a lot. I frowned at him. "Then we'll see what we can see and we will go from there."

"You mean, see if I'm a paraplegic or not." I gave him my best challenge look and was gratified by the way he seemed to pull back physically.

"Well, we hope it doesn't come to that. You're young and you're stronger and fitter than most people.

There's still a pretty good chance we'll get you walking. With luck, you might even ski competitively again."

I told myself not to grab onto his words as though they were a life raft. Hope, though, hope has a strange way of floating up. "What kind of chances are we talking about?"

Dr. Reynolds sighed. "It's early to tell."

"Give it a try."

He cleared his throat. "Of walking? Probably sixty-forty. Of skiing? Smaller. But if you walk out of here, and if the damage is minimal and if you lie still in the meantime, you stand a better chance."

"That's a whole lot of ifs," I said.

"I've got one more for you. If anyone can come back, it's you. You're a champion."

The words, meant to help me deal, stung like salt in an open wound, mostly because an ugly voice in my head answered back—

You were a champion. Past tense, Mia.

Creech

After my accident in Grindlewald, I'd been pissed at the world for a long time. Even when I came home to recuperate, I remember being such a jerk that my dad took me aside and said I better stop making my mother's life a misery, or I'd have to find somewhere else to live while I healed. He was right, but it still took a lot of soul searching to get past my anger and hurt and figure out my life. So I got it, why she was acting as she had. Then again, I'd never faced down possible paralysis and that was harder to imagine.

I wanted to go back to the hospital and tell her I would love her and I'd take care of her no matter what. It didn't matter to me, is what I'd tell her. But the truth was, it did matter. And if Mia ended up in a wheelchair, I was pretty sure she'd push me away further. She wasn't the kind of woman who would allow herself to be taken care of by anyone.

The Super G went off on schedule, though the entire team, coaches and competitors alike, went through it by rote. It was still cold as hell and the course was icy. Super G had always been Mia's best event, she would have loved those conditions. Without her, we didn't do well. Rachel managed a twelfth place, which wasn't terrific for her, but better than the rest of the team. Mary finished at the bottom of the standings, which was a bad showing, even for her. She had a fit at the finish line, calling bullshit conditions and throwing her helmet before stomping off. I was in no mood for adolescent tantrums. I caught up to her in the warm up area. I should have talked to her in private, but I was pissed, at our results, at Mia's accident, at the whole damn season.

"You have got to stop with the unsportsmanlike conduct," I said. The room was full of racers, and quite a few of them heard me, though I hadn't raised my voice. She pulled off her boots and didn't answer me. "I mean it, Mary. I will suspend you if you pull another tantrum like you did this afternoon."

That got her to look up. "Maybe you should take a look at your own behavior first. Like fucking Mia Whitmeyer. Or is that accepted conduct?"

I was so taken aback I didn't know what to say. I counted to ten. "You're out. Rest of the meet."

"You can't do that!"

"Watch me." I knew there would be repercussions. We were already down our best racer; we couldn't afford to lose another. I didn't much care. I saw Rachel staring at me as I left the room, so I stopped, handed her the keys to the rental. "Be back by nine," and then I walked out the door.

Mia

If I wasn't quite ready to latch onto hope, my parents were ready to do it on my behalf. They'd talked to Dr. Reynolds, too. "You're going to get through this,

Mia," said my dad, always willing to cheer me on.

I tried to smile, but couldn't quite manage it. An imaginary coin kept tossing in my head—tails I win, heads I lose. "I can't have a phone here, but I'm going to climb the walls if I have to lay here for six weeks with nothing but Austrian TV."

"See, you're restless already," said my mom. "That's a terrific sign."

"What about we get you an iPad?" my dad asked.

"I don't know about connections and such here."

"I'll get it figured for you." Already, he was a man on a mission. He liked having something to do, I couldn't much blame him. I wished I had more to do.

My mom picked up one of the cards from a well-wisher. The room had blossomed with cards and flowers and trinkets as though some crazed wizard had come along. I knew I should feel grateful, but in truth, it made me feel obliged, like I had to walk out of here tomorrow, grab my skis and win every race between now and the finish in Zermatt. I had already disappointed myself, I hated disappointing anyone else on my behalf. "Could we do something with all this stuff? It's a little overwhelming," I said.

"It shows how much people care about you, Mia," said my mom.

"They don't even know me." I caught her look and knew she wouldn't like my take on it. "Maybe we could give them to somebody? I'm sure there are folks here in the hospital without flowers. Maybe we could pass them on." I really just wanted them out of here, but I knew I could appeal to her generosity. And give her something to do.

My dad went off to figure out Internet connections and my mom went off to figure out how to donate gifts and flowers. I shut my eyes, thinking maybe I'd get the nurse to give me some extra pain meds so I could fall asleep, when Rachel and Reni walked in through the door.

"The meet is shit without you," said Rachel, a

forced happiness in her voice and then a pained look because she must have thought she'd said too much. I was in no mood to make her feel better.

"We miss you," said Reni, which was a platitude and wasn't helping with the strain.

"Mary Tyco had a major hissy fit. Coach suspended her," said Rachel, who seemed to be trolling around for something to say.

This was news, anyway. "What did she do?"

"She posted the worst time in the history of Super G. She knew it, everybody knew it, so she pulled off her helmet at the finish and threw it into the crowd. She nearly hit somebody with it," said Reni.

"She is such a little shit," Rachel added. For a minute, I almost forgot I was flat on my back in the hospital as her comment made me laugh.

My mom, who had begun moving flowers out of the room, came back in. "You girls sound like you're having a nice visit," she said. "The nurses are happy to redistribute these things, if you're sure." Mom took Joel bear from the side table.

"Leave him," I said. "I kind of like him. Coach gave him to me."

My mom nodded. "Well, that was thoughtful of him."

Rachel stood glancing sidelong at Reni as my mom left with some of the flowers. She glanced at the door. "About Coach—"

"Rachel, don't," said Reni.

"Don't what?" I asked.

"It's just a stupid rumor. Mary Tyco was mad and she wanted to stir up trouble," said Reni.

"Well, now you've got to tell me."

Rachel took a breath. "Mary accused Coach of sleeping with you."

"She's a shit," said Reni. "And she's been a little hinky, I guess we all have, since your accident."

"But the rumor is true, isn't it?" Rachel asked as my mom breezed back in. Rachel waited until she'd left again. "I mean, it makes sense, there's this vibe between you two. And then he misses races so he can be here. I might have chalked it up to his being nice, Coach Marv might have done the same given...And then I thought about it some more. That night in Cortina."

"That night in Cortina," I repeated. It seemed a million years ago. I took the bear off the table and held him. I should have told them it was a mistake, but I couldn't lie about it, not to them and not to myself either. "It doesn't matter anyway. Things have changed a lot."

"You? What about Italian Marco?" asked Reni.

"I sent him home. That night. He kissed me and I knew you guys were right, it was a really bad idea. And then I went with another, equally bad idea."

"You're not the first woman to sleep with a coach." said Rachel. "Besides, it was a one-night stand."

"Except you're in love with him, aren't you?" asked Reni.

"Right now, I don't know how I feel about much of anything." It was true, though not honest. I did love Creech, that's why it hurt so much to have to let him go. "Look, you've got to make sure he doesn't lose his job. What happened was as much my fault as his. More so, I came on to him."

"I doubt they'll fire him," said Reni. "You're both adults. And everything that's happened—and besides, if you're in love, it's all good, right?"

It would be all great, in the perfect fairy-tale world of my dreams it was great. Real life was a different story.

Creech

After my run in with Mary, I'd gone up to my room and thrown on my sweats and sneakers and gone out for a long run through Innsbruck's streets. It was dark out, days ended early this time of year, and if it had been cold with the sun out, it was bitter now. Each breath was like gasping in broken glass, the air searing my lungs. I invited the breathless pain, I coveted it.

Mia was in the hospital, her career likely over. In part, it was my fault. I had distracted her, I had caused this.

It was late by the time I got back to the hotel. I'd told Rachel and Reni to be back by nine and it was well past that by now. I should have gone to check they'd come in, I guess, but they were grown women, they could be responsible for themselves.

I took a shower and put on a pair of shorts and a T-shirt and climbed into bed. Tomorrow, we'd run the GS. The days seemed an endless loop of skiing and course setting and going to the next mountain and the next. This was the life I'd chosen, the one I would have asked for given a choice of any life I wanted. And I didn't know if I could do it anymore, I didn't even know if I wanted to. I felt as though I were as much in limbo as Mia.

There was a knock on the door as I turned down the bed. Davey was in the hall, he wasn't someone I wanted to see, but I figured I might as well set him straight. "I know. About earlier, about me and Mia. We should talk, I guess."

"Mary's gone," he said.

"What do you mean she's gone?"

"I mean she's not in her room. Lara says she was really upset and finally lit out. It was already after ten."

"Well, Jesus, she couldn't have gone far. She doesn't have a car." I thought of Rachel and Reni and my rental. They wouldn't be dumb enough, or irresponsible enough, to hand my rental over to Mary. I put on my sneaks and went to Rachel's room, at the far end of the hall, and knocked on the door.

She answered in her own version of shorts and T-shirt sleepwear, her toothbrush in hand. "Have you got my keys?" I asked.

"I left them by your door."

I cursed under my breath.

"Something wrong?"

"Mary's gone. Lara says she took off."

"Oh shit, you don't think?"

"That's exactly what I think. Where the hell would she go?"

Mia

As much as I wanted my folks here to hold my hand and prop me up, I knew this was a road I'd have to take alone. I wasn't a kid anymore, and they had their own lives to get back to. I broached the subject before they left for the night.

"We cancelled out for a couple of weeks," said my dad, as though it were no big deal to close an inn in the middle of the busy ski season.

"You can't just close up for six weeks," I said.

"It's not important," said my mom. "We're not leaving you here all alone."

I couldn't say anything else, though I knew at some point I'd have to convince them it would be fine to go.

After they left for the night, I picked up the bear. "Sweet dreams, Joel," Creech hadn't come by, probably because of the way I'd sent him off yesterday. It was for the best, anyway. He, too, had his own life to think about.

I heard a commotion in the hall and then Mary Tyco was standing by my bed. I thought, for a minute, I was hallucinating, but the nurse came breezing in. "No visitors now," she said in halting English, ready to escort Mary out.

I shook my head, still not sure this wasn't an illusion. If it wasn't, I wanted to know why Mary was there. "It's okay. Eine par minuten," I said in halting German, hoping it meant a few minutes.

The nurse frowned but seemed to understand. "Five minute," she said holding up her outstretched hand to illustrate.

Mary watched the nurse leave and then looked at

me as though I had contracted ebola and traction might be catching. She sniffed in and I realized she'd been crying. Last thing I needed was to have to console a crying teenager. I couldn't even console myself.

"It's pretty messed up, huh?' she said.

She looked so vulnerable that I was nearly able to forget what a pain in the ass she'd been. "Yeah, it is." A big part of me wanted to ask her what she thought she had to cry about. She had her whole career ahead of her. She would probably replace me. "Look, kid. You're not me. And you had nothing to do with this. You've got nothing to worry about."

She shook her head. "I'm thinking about quitting the team. I just—I'm not doing them any good."

"I can't believe you'd quit. You're not a quitter." It was the kind of thing I might have said to myself not so long ago.

She started to cry, hard. When she caught her breath, she said, "I messed things up, I messed them up bad. And now I can't look at Coach anymore."

"Because of this afternoon?"

She looked at me like I might be psychic. "I was going to apologize, but he wasn't there. The rental keys were sitting on the floor by the door, so I took the car. I guess I came to say I'm sorry."

"Does he know where you are? Does anybody?" She shook her head. "Jesus, they're probably worried about you. You have to go back."

Creech

We were ready to call the hospitals and police even though Mary had only been gone for an hour, maybe two. Even given the shitty day I'd had, losing her was on the top of the shit list.

"Airports? Train station?" Davey was thinking aloud. "Does she have some boy she can't wait to see again, wouldn't be the first time." He gave me an unreadable look that made me want to defend myself.

"I don't think there's anybody," said Rachel, she and Lara had come down to join in the search, which hadn't really become any kind of a search just yet.

"Maybe up to the hill?" I was thinking about my own run, the need to get away. I was about to get dressed again and wander back outside when the lobby doors opened and Mary waltzed in as though nothing were wrong. A wave of relief came over me, and a second later I was ready to strangle her, especially after she handed me the car keys as though it was no big deal. "Where the hell have you been?"

"Does it matter? I'm not racing tomorrow, remember? You pulled me off the team."

"Of course it matters. It's nearly midnight." I held up the keys. "You stole my car."

"I borrowed it." She gave me a defiant look, daring me to do something else to her. I'd already suspended her two races and there wasn't much else I could have done save expel her from the team. I was not ready to do that.

"Go upstairs. Go to bed and don't do it again, or I will personally buy you a plane ticket home."

"I went to visit Mia," she said. "I wanted to tell her I was sorry." Mary looked at her boots as though they had done her wrong. She was just a kid. Had I forgotten how hard competing on a world stage was when you were barely old enough to leave home without supervision? Mary, like most of the girls, had grown up fast.

I took Mary's arm and took her aside. "I'm sorry, too. I lost my temper and I shouldn't have. But next time, please ask before just taking off, okay?"

"Maybe there won't be a next time." She looked at me with tears in her eyes. "I thought about buying a ticket home myself. So maybe I should just let you do it."

"I'd rather you didn't. We need you, Mary. You're part of this team."

She looked like she didn't quite believe it. But

then she nodded. "Okay, I'm going to get some sleep." As I watched her walk off to the elevator, I thought about how much skiing had cost her, how much it had cost Mia. Oh, there were fabulous moments. All the girls, all the coaches, thought skiing was the best thing they had ever done or would ever do. I doubt any one of us would trade our lives for another, but the life we'd all chosen came with a price.

The rest of the meet went badly for us. I met with the girls afterward and tried to give them the 'We'll do better in Kitzbuhel and it's a long season,' speech, but my heart wasn't in it and neither were theirs.

Mia filled my thoughts, though I hadn't been in touch with her since she asked me to leave. Despite the rumors threatening to ruin my career, I wanted to shout to the world that I was in love with Mia Whitmeyer and the job I'd spent my whole life working to get wasn't worth giving her up for.

I told Davey I'd drive myself up to Kitzbuhel. "I can keep the rental. It's only an hour and I want to see how Mia's doing."

He gave me another guarded look. "I shouldn't be telling you what to do, Creech, but—"

"You're right. I'm a big boy. I can make my own decisions." I let it go at that.

Her mom and dad were with her when I came in, the three of them bent over an iPad. Her dad looked up. "Coach, I thought you'd be in Kitzbuhel."

"Yeah, I'm leaving right after this. I just wanted to stop in beforehand. To say goodbye." It wasn't the truth, really. Goodbye was the last thing I wanted to say.

Mia's mom took her husband's arm. "Why don't we get some coffee, Alex?" Her dad looked me over again, as though trying to figure out if I was as much a problem for Mia as her being in traction in a hospital several thousand miles from home.

"It's all good, Dad." Mia held up the iPad. "We'll

figure out the Facetime thing when you come back.

"Facetime?" I asked as they left.

Mia put the iPad on the side table. The bear I'd bought for her was still there. "My dad thought Facetime might keep me from climbing the walls."

"That's a good sign, right? You're ready to climb the walls?"

Her face darkened. "Please do not give me the 'you are a champion and everybody knows you'll be back to win all the gold at Sochi' speech. I've heard it enough and I couldn't stand hearing it from you."

"You are going to be okay, Mia. I know it."

"I'm scared as hell." She had tears in her eyes and blinked to chase them away.

I took her hand. "Of course you're scared. You'd have to be stupid not to be."

She ran her finger along the space between my thumb and forefinger. "I've had too much time to think, you know?"

"Yeah, I've been doing a lot of that, too. This whole thing has turned my life upside down. And the idea of leaving you here—" I bit my lip, last thing I wanted was to get all emotional.

"You've got to go, though. It's okay, I get it. The team needs you. You need a good season."

"I don't give a shit, that's the problem. Not like we're going anywhere in the standings without you anyway. None of it matters anymore."

She let go of my hand. "I have to believe the last ten years of my life meant something, whatever the next ten bring."

"I didn't mean it that way."

"You've got to go, Creech. Get on with it. You came to say goodbye, so say it already."

No, I wanted to say, not goodbye. Never goodbye, but I couldn't find the right words.

Fourteen

Mia

I could almost convince myself that, when the bus left for Kitzbuhel, I'd be on it. It wasn't until they all left that the finality of my situation set in. I wasn't going anywhere and I missed them, I missed skiing, with a longing as big as the world.

I got the iPad set up and tuned in Wi-Fi, so I could communicate with the world outside my hospital room. It would have been a great thing, except I didn't feel much like communicating. Communicating meant I'd have to put on a happy face, I'd have to say I was doing fine when, really, I wasn't. My dad was a big fan of Facetime, we used it when I was racing—cell phone connections were wonky and expensive in Europe and so we relied on the Internet systems at our hotels. Most of them had a designated room with a few computers set up and lots of those computers had Facetime or Skype, so we could see and talk to each other in real time.

He and Mom insisted on calling the family and so I had these guarded conversations with my brother and my aunts and uncles. I knew they just wanted to see for themselves that I was okay, but honestly, the nice and fine of it was exhausting and I was always glad when the Facetime was over. I wasn't quite as careful with my parents, though I wasn't exactly straightforward either. I didn't let on how I'd fallen into this deep well of apathy, where one day was pretty much like the last.

I spent the balance of my time playing video games. They were dumb as hell, save the puppy and the candy factory, but with them, I could numb my mind and dull my senses and keep myself from thinking too hard on scary things, like what the future might hold.

I wrote e-mail to the other girls on the team and to Tin, again trying to keep it upbeat. I told them German TV sucked and I wished they had *The Bachelor*. I told them about the bad food, and that they had Jell-O even in Austrian hospitals, who knew? I tried to write Creech a couple of times, but just couldn't.

Tin wrote me and said she'd love to do Facetime and I ignored the e-mail for a week and then finally worked up enough gumption to set it up. I pasted on a smile and hit the button and there she was, looking the same as always, on the other side of my computer screen. It wasn't up close and in person, which was a good thing, because without the screen between us I would have been an emotional wreck. Funny, how a computer screen and a few thousand miles were the glue holding me together.

Still, a big lump lodged in my throat and I had to swallow hard to get it down again. There was a softness around her eyes and looking at them made the lump come back up, so I focused on her lips instead. "Hey, girl." I said.

"Hey, Ice."

I managed to hang on to the fake smile for a few more seconds, though by then I knew damn well it was futile and Tin began swimming away as my eyes got ready for a good cry. "So," I said to cover up the emotions. "I hear you're having a baby."

Tinny didn't laugh, she didn't even smile. "I'm worried about you."

"I'm going to be fine, Tin. A few more weeks and I'll be back in New Hampshire. Twenty-two days and four hours until, fingers crossed, I move on out. I'm getting tired of hospital food, so this is a damn good thing."

"Nothing yet, though, with the paralysis?"

Leave it to Tin to shoot for the heart. I'd spent the last few weeks either testing my toes to see it they'd move (they didn't) or trying to forget I even had toes.

"No. The doctor says it's too early to tell. 'Dees tings time take,' he says."

"He's right, you know. And I know patience isn't your strongest trait. But you'll get through this."

"How's my God baby?" I needed, desperately, to change the subject. I prayed that Tin would let me.

"She's a she, did I tell you? The last ultrasound found no sign of a scrotum. We might call her Mia, though I'm leaning toward Kanga, because she kicks like a little kangaroo." Tin turned sideways so I could see her baby bump.

"You coming back? After?" I asked.

Tin turned forward again, her face all serious. "I don't think so, Mia. Racing, it was huge for me. But I think it's time for me to move on. Jack and this little girl-bean I'm carting around, they're bigger than racing, you know?"

I didn't know, not really. I couldn't imagine a life without racing. Everything, everyone I knew was connected to me by a pair of skis. Creech, especially Creech, was connected to me through racing.

To Tinny, I said, "Yeah, I guess they would be," and I told her to take care of herself and I promised to see her when I could. And as her image disappeared from my screen, I felt more alone than ever.

Creech

After Innsbruck and then Kitzbuhel, the job I couldn't wait to get up for in the morning turned into a chore, into time I had to endure. I went through the motions, I did my job because I had to and what else could I have done? But every day I spent skiing down a hill or setting up gates for a slalom run, every time I stood in the start house giving pep talks to my racers as they faced down the hill, I thought of Mia. I thought of her streaking over the snow like a rocket, her speed, her agility, like a work of art. There was an excitement around her when she raced, it was nearly touchable. It was sexy as hell, watching Mia race was like making love to her. She was passionate about skiing and her passion showed in every turn she carved.

Skiing was Mia's first love, maybe her only love, probably more fulfilling than a relationship with any man could ever be. Given a choice between me and skiing, she would choose skiing without thinking twice. She had chosen it, in fact, when she'd left me alone in my bed in Cortina.

It made me wonder if Connor had split because he knew he couldn't compete with a steep slope and a pair of skis. The damndest part was, her obsession with skiing wouldn't have made me leave. I understood her passion, or thought I did, because it matched my own.

Her accident had turned everything inside out and, in some way I didn't fully understand, it had taken my passion for fast snow and swallowed it down whole. It didn't help that the team was falling apart. Without Mia and Tin Reaton, we'd lost our best hopes for capturing any World Cup medals. Rachel and Reni and the other girls were good, but they wouldn't be able to beat out the powerhouse stars on the other teams. They couldn't fill the hole left in Mia's absence and they knew it.

I did try to work up enthusiasm. This was my life, after all, and I tried not to think beyond the next race and then the next. Time dragged and this was a new sensation for me. I tried, about a hundred times, to e-mail Mia. I'd go down, get on the computer in the hotel and type in her address. Then I'd stare at the screen. Once or twice, I managed to type a few lines—'How are you? We all miss you.' The words sounded so trite I could nearly taste them, like metal in my mouth, and I deleted them and stared some more until the people waiting for a turn at the screen started shuffling their feet or clearing their throats and I'd get up and walk away.

It went on like that for the rest of the winter. After an eternity of time, we got ready to travel from Grenoble, in France, over the mountains to Zermatt, in Switzerland, for the World Cup finals. We had little chance of medaling in anything—Rachel had a small chance of making the podium in downhill, but anything else would have taken a miracle.

I was looking for miracles, but they had little to do with Zermatt. Over through another few mountain passes, in another Alpine town west of us, Mia was getting ready to shed her casts like a second skin. I knew this not because I'd finally written to her, but because Reni had told me. She sat next to me on the bus to Zermatt and said it casually, in the way conversations were often made on these long bus rides. "Looks like Mia is finally getting out of traction," she said.

"Great, isn't it?" I said, as though I really had known it all along.

Reni gave me a funny look. "She said she hasn't heard from you. I asked her."

She raised her eyebrows, daring me to continue my lie. I thought it best to come clean. "I guess I don't know what to say to her." I pretended to look at the mountains that surrounded us as we wound through the pass. "She asked me to go on with my life and to take care of the team, so I'm doing that."

Reni scoffed. "I thought you were one of those men who understood women. She asked you to go, but that's not what she wanted."

"I don't understand women," I turned back to her and tried to smile, though I fell short. "Besides, Mia is not your ordinary woman."

"Which is why you love her."

I thought she'd meant love her as in 'we all love her', as in 'I love ice cream'. "We do all love her."

Reni sighed. "Yes, we do. But you're the only one of us in love with her." I didn't know what to say to that. "You need to tell her how you feel. I'm pretty sure she feels the same way."

I'd known Reni since she was a kid, when I

coached her in the junior levels, and I knew she could be a bit of a romantic. "I need to respect her boundaries, Reni. That's all."

"You haven't written her in six weeks, Coach. That's not respect for boundaries. She misses you, I guarantee it."

"I don't know what to say. I'm no good at letters, e-mail or otherwise."

"Then maybe you ought to go see her." Reni raised her brows again, a challenge. If only she knew how much I wanted to. But I couldn't, not now. Then again, in a week, the racing season would be over and we'd get a well-deserved break. There was no reason I couldn't stay in Europe a little longer.

Mia

My mom and dad stayed on in Innsbruck. I knew they were sacrificing a lot. The inn they owned in Franconia couldn't run with them away and that meant missing out on the busy ski season. Every time I brought this up, my dad would say that I was the reason they were able to stay in business. There was some truth to this, I guess, being a racer of some renown made people want to stay in the place I grew up, though actually my parents' house was a quarter mile down the road and I didn't live in Franconia anymore. I was too tired and caught up in my own wreckage to argue much, though I did hope I wouldn't be the reason for their bankruptcy.

I did think about home, of going back with my parents and living with them for a while, which would be the most obvious option once I got out of rehab at Dartmouth. I didn't love the idea, and I certainly didn't want to think about what the future would hold.

Then my mom came up, inadvertently, with another reason to dread a homecoming. My dad had gone out for a walk. I got my restlessness from him, I'd begun to realize, and the hospital room would drive both of us insane. My mom stayed behind. She'd taken up knitting and she was attempting to make a sweater and failing at it badly. She'd undone her stitches four times and was unraveling yet again. I joked that sweater-making might not be her thing and she smiled and then turned serious as she reloaded the knitting needles. "I spoke to Connor." She said it casually, as though she'd said, "I could use a cup of coffee," and I thought I'd misheard her at first.

"You talked to him?"

She nodded as she cast stitches. "He called the hotel. He wanted to know how you were and didn't want to e-mail you, because he thought it would be awkward."

Awkward didn't begin to cut it. "And what did you say?"

She shrugged, like it was no big deal. "I told him about the spinal shock, your prognosis." She looked up from her knitting. "He deserved to know, Mia."

"Why? Last I checked he was getting married to someone else."

"He was practically part of the family. You were with him for a long time."

"Okay, so now he knows." It really wasn't that big a deal, was it?

"He asked if he could come see you, in Hanover. He wanted to know if you'd be okay with it. I told him it would be fine."

"You what?" I didn't know how to process this. The truth was I hadn't given Connor a second thought since my accident. I hadn't been thinking about him much before my accident, either. And this was a good thing; I'd guess it meant I was truly over him. Yet the idea of him calling, of him coming to see me, stirred up something.

"He still cares about you, Mia." I had nothing else to say. If this had happened to him, I would want to know, too. I'd probably go visit him, too.

Still, it was disturbing. Because there was

something else I knew—in all of the years we'd been together, I'd never loved Connor as much as he'd loved me. He'd been there for me at every turn; he celebrated every victory and commiserated every defeat. I hadn't been there for him. I'd taken him for granted. And, though I thought he was the love of my life, and everyone else assumed he was, the truth was, he wasn't and never had been.

I met Connor when I was fifteen, when we were both racing in the junior divisions at Cannon Mountain. I was being called a rising star even then, I won a lot, so often, in fact, that it became common place. Even so, I knew it was a tough road to the Olympics, like to being a high school baseball or basketball star wanting a spot on a major league team. The road was my obsession, I stoked that dream with all the ambition I had, and I had a truck load of ambition.

Most of the kids I knew were this way, fiercely competitive, focused, with a love of skiing as fast as the snow and the vertical drop would allow. Connor, though, was different. Connor was, compared to the rest of us, downright laid back.

He came to his skiing talents naturally—his dad was a ski instructor at a nearby area called Wild Cat and his mom had skied competitively in college. He was a natural, too, to watch him was to imagine he came out of his mother's womb with skis attached to his feet.

I remember the first time I saw him. We were all of us getting ready for our first team practice. It was early in the season, late November, and a few of the oaks that lined the slopes still had a few stray brown leaves attached to the branches. Snow comes early and often in the White Mountains of New Hampshire and that year, we'd been especially blessed (or cursed, depending how you looked at it) with an early snow storm that had covered everything in a thick white blanket. The snow at Cannon was powder soft, a rare treat, and we were all of us ready to get into it. There was time for a warm up run (a fun run, the coaches called it) and so we went up to the top and came streaking down, just enjoying the day.

I was standing along the side of the slope with my friend Liza Albrook. She and I had discovered boys and our new infatuation was watching the guys on the team and deciding whether or not any of them were worth pursuing. A few of them we'd been in school with since grade school and, though they'd grown out of boyhood into a more appealing adolescence, they were far too familiar. So we concentrated on kids from other schools and towns. Connor was one of those.

The hill, a steep run called DJ's Tramline that ran under the tramway, had been carved into moguls by skiers turning their skis in the soft snow the day before. Because it was a 'black diamond' expert-level trail, the maintenance crews didn't run the snow cat over it to smooth them out. Most of the kids, and especially the boys, were into riding the moguls hard and fast. I think they were probably as infatuated as we were and spent a lot of time showing off.

Connor skied past us, no poles, no helmet, a bandana around his neck, while playing a harmonica. The hill and moguls seemed a natural extension of his long legs and I watched, fascinated. I asked Liza if she knew who he was. She didn't. "I'm going to find out," I said.

He wasn't all that different from the rest of us, young and a little brash and fearless, but there was something about him—he lived the way he skied, as if life were a slope he could glide down with mindless ease. It's the same attitude that made him quit skiing competitively a few years after we met, he just didn't want to hassle. Though, despite his own lack of ambition for winning a place in ski history, he always supported my career. Until he didn't. I guess keeping a relationship with me got to be too much of a hassle, too.

Creech

The Zermatt meet finished and I still hadn't e-mailed Mia. It wasn't because I'd forgotten, getting in touch with her and being with her pretty much filled up my brain space. Everything about Zermatt reminded me of Val D'Isere all those years ago. We didn't do well, no one thought we would. Rachel missed the podium by a split second in the downhill, which would have been our only team victory. The almost win was especially hard to take.

I knew Reni was right, I couldn't avoid e-mailing Mia. I went down to the Wi-Fi area of our hotel the day we finished the last race. The season done, we were scheduled to fly into Kennedy in the morning, from where we'd all get some well-deserved time off. Nearly everyone staying at the hotel was connected to ski racing and they'd either packed up and left for home or gone off to party in the village.

I sat at the computer in the deserted room. The lights were off and I didn't bother to turn them on. Maybe it would be easier to pour my heart onto the computer screen in the dark. "Hi Mia," I began and then nearly deleted the line. I forced myself to continue. "I hear you got your casts off today. I wish I could be there with you. I have a notion to drive all night to see you."

I stared at the words. It was as though I'd written the message to myself. I deleted it. Then I went to the hotel desk and rented a car.

I went to Davey's room, knowing he would be out with the rest of the coaches. I left a note under his door, saying I wouldn't be flying back with the team, I was going to Innsbruck. Davey hadn't been wild about being overlooked for the head coach position. It hadn't been my decision, but there was an argument to be made that the job should have gone to him—he'd been with the team for a few years whereas I was coaching young racers in development. He'd been nothing but fair, and though I knew he didn't approve of what had happened between Mia and me, he'd not made any complaint about it, either privately or officially.

It was five and half hours over the mountains to where she was. It was after midnight by the time I drove away from the hotel. I really would be driving all night.

Fifteen

Mia

All my life, I've been tuned into my body. Conditioning was important as a racer, but it was more than that, I was proud of what my body could do. I trained hard—weight training for strength, running for endurance, yoga for flexibility. Lying still for six weeks was as though I was suspended in space and there was nothing I could do about it and nowhere I could go.

Because my body wasn't doing as it was supposed to, I prepared for the worst. Pessimism wasn't something I ascribed to, normally I was sure of myself, if I failed I tried harder, worked harder, until I could succeed. Being a paraplegic would be a disaster for me, but if it was going to happen, I was going to be the best damn paraplegic who ever lived. I started reading up on wheelchair athletes. I made a list of ski programs for the disabled. Maybe being prepared would keep the worst from happening; the way carrying an umbrella seemed to keep the rain away.

My first few weeks in the hospital, I checked in with my toes every day. They ignored all my commands and signals. After a while, I stopped trying to force the issue. I'd forget them like they had forgotten me. I concentrated on my arm strength instead, working with a physical therapist to isolate the muscles in my shoulders and arms and keep them from atrophy.

My folks didn't want to hear about wheelchairs and paraplegic athletes. They wanted to concentrate on full recovery. I couldn't do that, full recovery was beyond my control and beyond my control had never been part of my vocabulary.

As the countdown to my being released from the suspended animation of my traction wound down, I became anxious. I would have to face my fate straight on; I was about to walk to my execution or get a stay.

Dr. Reynolds had, after consulting and agreeing with the Austrian doctor's treatment plan for me, gone back to Salt Lake City and left me with Dr. Schuler, who I privately renamed Dr. Frankenstein. Childish, I knew, but I felt some need to defend myself and he was the closest thing to an arbiter of my future.

He came to see me the afternoon before the casts were due to come off. "We will first do the MRI, to see how all has healed, yes?" Had he been a bit more demonstrative, I might have imagined him yelling "surprise!" and offering up a birthday cake. In fact, my thirtieth birthday was only a few months away, which didn't help my sense of impending doom. If my accident didn't end my career, age would do it soon enough.

"What are the chances all is healed?" I decided I would be calm and intelligent in facing my personal firing squad, even as my innards screamed at me.

"Oh, very good. Excellent, I think."

I wanted to take this in and dance around with it. I wouldn't let myself. "I still can't feel my toes." I tried to wiggle them in illustration, concentrating like I always did. Nothing happened at first, and then, slowly, my big toe gave a nod. Sometime, when I hadn't been paying attention, my feet had walked back to me and made a connection. "Hey." There were tears in my eyes and I let out a sob.

My mother, who had been standing at the foot of the bed with my dad, was at my side in an instant. I think she feared I'd finally crashed and burned. "Honey, it's okay."

"They work," I whispered when I found my voice. I made it happen again, and again, it took all my concentration to do.

"Your toes moved." My mother's eyes filled with tears and then my dad was at my side and the three of us were crying like children.

Dr. Schuler quickly threw a bucket of cold water on our euphoria-fest. "It is a hopeful sign, yes."

I let go of my mother's hand, ready to expel the doctor from the room for not jumping up and down with happiness. "What, exactly, do you mean a hopeful sign?"

"It means you're sailing towards a full recovery," said my dad. He, too, didn't want to let go of joy quite so fast.

Schuler cleared his throat. "This can be so, yes."

"But?" If he was going to spoil things, might as well have it.

"This depends on the condition of the spine, yes? How much is the nerve damage. It can be a complete recovery, but this can be also partial, the reversal of the paralysis."

"It will be complete," my father insisted.

I wasn't so sure. It took a lot of concentration to move. Maybe a partial recovery was the best I could hope for.

Creech

I hadn't been sleeping well, thinking about Mia and the team and my future whenever my head hit the pillow. The season had taken a toll on me and by rights I should have ended up falling asleep at the wheel and careening headlong into an Alpine ravine along the winding highway. But the thought of seeing Mia again sustained me and gave me energy. I rolled down the window and let the cold night air slap me around, found a rock station on the radio and cranked up the volume enough to blast away any remnants of sleepiness. I drove as fast as I dared, determined to get there in record time. It was five o'clock in the morning when I hit the Innsbruck city limit.

No hospital would allow visitors before the sun was fully up. I parked the car in the hospital visitor lot and tried to figure out what to do. After having broken the sound barrier to get here, I had too much time on my hands.

There wasn't much open at that hour, so I wandered up and down the cobbled streets for a while. The air was cold and still and the sky had taken on a rosy glow as the new day dawned. The chalet style houses common in this part of the world often had murals painted on them and I stopped to look at one now. A band of angels rose on clouds and I wondered if the painter had intended to show off his work in this light, because the picture had a heavenly cast to it. The sun rose and light flooded into the narrow street, illuminating the cobbles. The mountains stood in dark relief beyond. I wasn't a guy who believed in portent, but this seemed a good sign, as though the world were saying everything was going to be just fine.

Then, as though the universe was not yet done with the message, a tall figure came walking towards me. It was hard to make out under the glare of the newborn sun, but I could see that the person was waving at me. I thought for one spellbound second it was Mia. It wasn't of course, though it was someone I was nearly as surprised to see—Katya Hofstadter.

It shouldn't have been all that surprising, Katya lived in Innsbruck. Still, the last race of the season for the women had been contested less than twenty-four hours before in Zermatt. Katya hadn't medaled in the event, though she had been good enough overall to earn her fourth World Cup title. Nearly as impressive as Mia's six, I might have teased her in better circumstances.

"Creech," She gave me a hug, greeting me like an old friend. The racing community was a small one, and friendships developed between all the skiers. I know Mia was fond of Katya and the feeling was mutual. "You are in Innsbruck." She said it as a statement, but there was a question in it.

"You are too." I answered with my own fact-turned-question.

"Ach, ja. I want to come home. So I leave after the

race yesterday. Too much, how you say it? Crazy?"

I nodded. "Crazy. We call it hoopla at my house."

Katya smiled. "Hoopla. Yes, this word I like." She raised an eyebrow and I knew she wanted to know what I was doing here. "You drive here, today?"

"I drove all night."

I didn't know if I wanted to, or if I could, explain it any better than that. Katya saved me from myself. She pointed out a building on the far side of the street. "I am going to the bakery, for broedchen. You come and we have café, yes?"

I followed her to the bakery. If the mural painter had captured a glimpse of heaven on the side of the chalet, the baker had captured its smell—fresh baked bread wafted out onto the cold morning air; a blast of it, warm and scented, hit us as we stepped into the shop.

"I live over two blocks," Katya said once she had the breakfast rolls in hand. "You come, yes?"

It was still early. "I don't want to intrude."

She made a face. "Heh, no. Is like you Americans say, no problem."

I walked with her to another chalet-style house, a wooden balcony over the front, Angels on the side of this one, too. "I love the murals," I said.

"Was here when we buy the house. Maria Himmelfahrt—How you say, Mary goes into the heaven? Is very like home here in Tyrol."

Hans Jorgen was making coffee when Katya and I walked into her kitchen. She said something to him in rapid German and he laughed and held out his hand. "Ja, Creech. Wilcomen."

Katya invited me to sit on the el-shaped bench by the wooden kitchen table. She put the rolls in a basket and then piled some cheese on a plate. "You have Austrian fruestueck today." Hans Jorgen poured some coffee and put cream and sugar on the table.

The generosity felt overwhelming, though maybe I was becoming emotional because of my lack of sleep. Katya said something else to Hans Jorgen and then sat down across from me. "You come to see Mia, yes?"

I shouldn't have been surprised that my being here was so easy to figure out, but I guess I was. "I couldn't leave for home without seeing her."

"It is a very terrible thing, what happen to her," Hans Jorgen said.

I nodded, not trusting my voice.

Katya, noticing my distress, said. "We come home early. To stay some time by us."

Hans Jorgen smiled at her and took her hand. "Katya, she is not so much liking the reporters. It is hard, sometimes. So we run away."

"Run away. I think I'd like to do that." I took a sip of coffee. "Maybe I did run away, from Zermatt."

"I think you are running in the right way, to Mia," said Hans Jorgen.

Mia

Despite all the trying to get myself to be real and face facts, a big part of me hoped, and could nearly believe, the casts would come off and I'd be good as new. I'd start running around Innsbruck and begin training for the next season and I'd win every gold medal contested in the next Olympics. Yup, that was the perfect movie plot fantasy and I wanted, very much, to believe in it.

Reality was a different story. The good news was that it looked as though I wouldn't be wheelchair bound, but my reflexes and muscle responses were slow and so being Olympic bound seemed a distant possibility.

Dr. Schuler came back the next morning after reading my MRI and my x-rays. He might as well have had a caution light attached to his head. Yes, both of my femurs, which had been fractured in the accident, had healed completely. The swelling in my back was gone and the odds were tipped heavily in favor of my getting full control of the muscles in the lower half of my body. But, and there was a big but attached to the good news,

I'd shattered my pelvis and my hip wasn't properly aligned, meaning hip replacement on both sides of my body. The hip surgery would keep me in the hospital an extra week or so.

I wasn't ever going to be best friends with Dr. Frankenstein but, after the accident, he had dragged me back from the edge of oblivion and in less capable hands I might well have ended up in a wheelchair. Innsbruck had one of the finest sports medicine facilities in the world and mine wasn't the first ski accident they'd treated. I'd landed here by a stroke of fate, or luck, if you could ever call such a thing lucky. "When do you want to do the surgery?" I asked.

"Soon as it is possible. Today, after we remove the casts."

So it was decided. The casts would come off and I'd have surgery. Then, after a few days, I'd be able to travel back to New Hampshire, to a rehab center in Dartmouth, where I'd remain for a few weeks or a few months, depending on how fast I could recover.

The cast cutter came and, with a few cuts of a special saw, I was set free from my cocoon. I felt light all over, I hadn't realized how I'd become used to the restrictions. It felt as though I would float away. Shortly after that I was wheeled away to face the next set of restrictions.

I woke up in recovery, Creech coloring my drug-induced dreams. I couldn't remember the details, only that it left me feeling a rosy glow, a nice counter to the ache in my pelvis, which felt as though someone was trying to cut their way out with a dull knife.

I was groggy, in and out of sleep, when they wheeled me back to my room. My dad was waiting for me, his face etched with worry. I thought about what an ordeal I'd put my parents through these past months and wished there was some way I could make up for it. I knew I never could.

"You came through like a champ," he said, kissing my forehead. He was a terrible liar, there was something else he wasn't saying. I needed to know what it was.

"What's wrong?"

"Nothing, sweetheart. You did well. It's just—it's been a long day." I waited for the shoe to drop. "There's someone here to see you." My thoughts jumped immediately to Creech and I wondered why Dad was so concerned. He didn't know about my relationship with Creech, though he might have figured it out. At any rate, he didn't really know Creech, so I didn't get why it would upset him.

In the few seconds it took for these thoughts to whir through my brain, my mom came through the door and behind her walked the someone. It wasn't Creech, but Connor.

Sixteen

Creech

I was on a plane bound for Kennedy by that evening. I called myself a coward and a fool; I was surely both of those things for not staying. The self-loathing didn't loosen the grip on my heart, which felt like it was in a vise, the life squeezed from it.

Hans Jorgen had driven me to the hospital after breakfast. "You will come stay with us, yes? While you are here?" he asked as he pulled into the visitors' lot.

I thought of him and Katya, the touches under the kitchen table meant to go unnoticed, the way he'd joked about running away. I imagined they had very little privacy on the circuit and I wouldn't impose on them to take away what little time they did have. "I made a reservation," I said, "But thank you for the offer."

He didn't offer twice, so I knew I'd made the right choice. "I wish you best of luck. I think you and Mia, very good together."

I smiled at his assessment as he drove off thinking: I love her more than you know. Though there was still a hint of fear. I wished I'd written her. Maybe my showing up out of the blue wasn't such a great idea, though it was too late to back out now.

Her room was empty when I got there and another moment of panic hit me as I wondered if I'd missed her altogether. I was told she was in surgery when I asked at the nurse's station and this sent up a yet another wave of panic—had something else gone wrong? The nurse wouldn't give me any other information and so I thought my best bet was to wait.

I passed the time, an hour or two of it anyway, by finding a room in a small guest house. Once checked in, I took a shower and lay down though sleeping was out of the question. On my way into the hospital a few hours later, I ran into Mia's surgeon. He probably knew who I was, but I reintroduced myself anyway as Mia's coach and asked about the surgery.

"It was very good. A success, I think." I nodded and waited expectantly. "She have the bilateral, both of the hips replaced. This takes a little longer, but she is very strong. I think she will be walking again very soon. Skiing? We must wait and see."

I thanked him, feeling much better. Hip replacement was something that had been mentioned as a possibility after her first surgery and didn't seem nearly as daunting as the possibilities that had been popping around in my head.

She was, Dr. Schuler told me, being wheeled back to her room as we spoke. I thought about being with her when she'd come out of the haze of anesthesia the last time. The time she'd said, "I love you." She could, of course, have been talking to anyone, she was on some heavy medication, but I chose to think she meant me. She had been looking at me when she said it.

I'd driven five hours through mountain passes in the middle of the night, walked ten kilometers through the wintery Innsbruck streets before dawn and rented a room while I waited for her to come out of surgery. And yet, I wanted to do something more, something concrete, to show how much I cared. I went to the gift shop and bought a single red rose. Cliché, I knew it, but I needed a romantic gesture, or maybe a prop. If I wasn't the "I love you" guy of Mia's dreams, I intended to become him.

I got off the elevator with flower in hand and walked down to her room. The door was open and she wasn't alone; inside were her parents and a tall blond man who was holding her hand. He glanced up and caught my eye. I walked past the room. The ward was circular and so I walked the long way around back to the elevator. In the lobby, I handed the rose to an elderly woman in a wheelchair. She was startled by the gesture and then grinned and put the petals to her nose to take in the fragrance. At least I had brightened someone's day. Then I got into my rental, went back to the guesthouse and repacked and drove to the airport.

I'd known who the guy was the instant I'd seen him. Connor O'Keefe, the man in all of Mia's pictures. The one she'd forgotten was in the family photo. Apparently, he hadn't forgotten.

Mia

The upset at seeing Connor, or maybe the wearing off of the anesthetic, made me woozy. I must have gone pale, because my dad asked if I was okay and Connor grabbed my hand and asked "Should I get a nurse?"

I took a deep breath and swallowed down a wave of nausea. "No." I pointed to the kidney shaped tray on the bed table as the nausea rose again. My mom passed me the tray and I threw up into it, managing to gross myself out and mortify myself in the same moment. My mom went into full mother mode, taking the tray and rinsing it, wetting a washcloth and wiping my mouth and face, asking if I wanted water or the tray back. "I'm good now," I answered. Then I added, "Sorry."

They, all three in unison, said it was fine. I wanted to close my eyes and make them disappear. "I guess I'm not up to company."

Connor took my hand again. "Could I have a minute? In private?"

My dad looked like he wanted to grab my ex-boyfriend and drag him from the room for even suggesting such a thing. "It's okay," I told him. It wasn't really. I was still woozy and I hurt, and Connor, who had been erased from my life, was holding my hand. The other thing was that I was confused as hell and I needed to find out what he thought he was doing here and that was a conversation better had without my parents in the room.

My mom took my dad's arm. "We can go get some coffee."

They went out for coffee more than was good for them and Dad was not so easily persuaded. "You sure?" I nodded and watched them go.

Connor started talking as soon as they were gone. "I bet you're wondering why I'm here."

I took my hand from his and scowled at him. He hadn't the right to be possessive. Not anymore.

"After you fell—I saw the tape, they kept showing it on Sports Center—and—I don't know. It broke me up. It felt like I was the one who'd fallen. I felt like I made a terrible mistake in letting you go."

Had he come to me the day after the fateful hike when he told me it was over; I would have taken him back in a heartbeat. Sure, I would have put up a fight, I'd been hurt and angry, but in the end I would have forgiven him. Now, though? I wasn't nearly as sure that taking him back wouldn't be the worst mistake I could make. He was standing by my bed, though, thousands of miles from home. Maybe I owed him something. What exactly?

"So you came to see me and I threw up on you. Romantic, isn't it?" I thought maybe I could make a joke of it, cover my anger, my pain, the nausea.

He grinned. "Not the first time you upchucked on me. Remember the prom?"

"Oh God. I still owe you a shirt." Connor lived in Gorham, which was about an hour north of my hometown. In high school, I had gone to his senior prom and he to mine. It was kind of a big deal and when his came, the O'Keefe's invited me to stay with them for the weekend. In typical prom night fashion, his friend Finn had made a concoction with a ton of booze and I'd gotten drunk and very sick.

So in the middle of the night, when we should

have been making out under the stars, I was bent over the O'Keefe's' guest bathroom toilet in my prom dress, with Connor holding my hair back. His shirt had sustained a dousing from me. I got to hand it to him, he stayed with me even though I was pretty sure my heaving made him want to heave himself.

"Kool-aide and vodka is a lethal combination," he said, taking my hand again.

"The garbage can Finn Ackley mixed it in should have been a tip-off," I said.

"First and last time we ever drank that shit."

The way he said 'we' reminded me of the couple we had been. The kids we weren't anymore. "Why are you here?"

"I told you."

"You have to figure out if breaking up was a mistake, so you flew to Austria."

Connor glanced away. "Almost. I had the opportunity to come to Austria. I'm up for a promotion. I might be moving here, actually."

Connor had given up racing competitively, but skiing was still part of his life. He was a sales rep for Fischer, an Austrian ski company. Their US headquarters were in New Hampshire, which was where Connor was based. Their corporate headquarters were in Reid, a town not far from Salzburg, a few hours west of Innsbruck.

"International sales?" I asked.

He nodded. "It's kind of a big deal. They wanted to talk to me and I couldn't come out here without coming to see you. So I took a couple of extra days."

It was a little less romantic, and maybe a little less needy, than flying to Austria just to see me. Still, he had taken extra time and driven several hours to see me. I wasn't sure how to feel about it when something else occurred to me. "What about Lynn?"

He looked surprised I knew the name of his fiancé. I hadn't known, actually, until Rachel looked her up on Facebook. Lynn Santini was twenty-three and worked at Fischer in the business office, Rachel had reported gleefully. "He traded a world class skier for an accountant? What is wrong with that boy?"

"I'd guess it's a great job," I'd said. "Free skis." I didn't know why I'd want to defend my ex's new love. I wasn't even sure I'd wanted to know her name.

"You can have all the freebies you want, Ice," Rachel had said. "You just snap your fingers and every sales rep between here and Tokyo will come bearing gifts of ski equipment." I'd laughed at her assessment. It was true, ski companies loved when I skied their product and they'd bend over backwards to get me to do it. If I'd said I wanted a pair of pink skis with purple polka dots, they would have made them for me. That was then, I reminded myself. That was before, past tense. The way I'd loved Connor, past tense.

"Lynn is—" Connor swallowed deeply. "Lynn is not sure she wants to move to Austria. Though it would only be for a couple of years."

"I'm sure she's not too wild about your coming to see me."

He looked away. "I told her I can't...that I need to figure things out. We have a lot of history, Mia. We—"

I held up my hand. I should have told him, then, that history needed to remain in the past. That he wasn't the one who invaded my dreams and my thoughts in all the quiet hours of the day. I glanced to the teddy bear, still on the bed stand. I'd told Creech what we had wasn't important, I'd sent him away. In six weeks, he hadn't been to see me, he hadn't tried to call or write. I felt vulnerable and alone. Connor was, once again as he always had been, here. So I didn't say those things to him. "How long can you stay?" I asked instead.

Creech

The tenants who had rented my house in Wilmington had moved out at the beginning of the month, so the house was currently empty. It seemed the perfect refuge. I'd go up there, I'd get myself together. Maybe I'd ask Bell if he was up to refinishing my kitchen cabinets with me, it was something we'd talked about.

I missed my old life, when I'd coached up and coming kids and lived in a place I thought of as home. Coaching on the FIS circuit was a huge opportunity and I felt like I'd won the lottery when I got the call. Now though, I wasn't sure it was a good fit. Just as Mia wasn't a good fit. No, that was a lie and there was no point in lying to myself. Mia and I were good together, we were close to perfect. The circumstances sucked—that she'd been so badly hurt, that she didn't seem to want me around, that she was back with Connor. I'd had my heart broken, once, by a woman who couldn't love me back the way I wanted. I couldn't do it again. I wouldn't. Since Connor was back in Mia's life, I'd bow out. Not because I was noble, but because I needed to protect myself.

I took a commuter flight to Albany, where my brother Eric waited to pick me up. We'd drive up to Ridge Run, to our parents' place, together. I'd stay for a day or two then borrow my dad's old truck and go to Wilmington. Eric had been a kid when I'd first left home and it always hit me when I saw him now, that he wasn't a kid anymore but a man in his mid-twenties. He was the only one of my brothers who expressed an interest in keeping the family ski area running and just then I wondered if he hadn't made the best choices of any of us.

He loaded my suitcases into the back of his Accord. "New car?" I asked. "You must be doing better than I thought."

He smiled. "Houses in Wells rent for cheap. I'm thinking of buying, but..." He stopped for a minute to merge onto traffic on the Northway. "First we need to make the business solid again."

"What do you mean solid again?" The business had always been small, but my folks and Mallory's dad, Harry Prescott, managed to eke out a living by filling a niche the corporate ski areas couldn't fill.

"We can't afford to run behind, or the corporate areas will swallow us. I'd like to build a new snowboard park. That little hill off to the side would be perfect. Our folks and Harry already share the deed to the land. Expensive, though, we'd need a new lift and more grooming equipment. Insurance would go up. Dad and Harry aren't so hot on taking on the extra debt, it's a risk. Mom, well, Mom is Mom."

"She thinks any idea her baby boy has is amazing."

Eric smiled. "Yeah, she always did like me best. Maybe because I'm not trucking through Europe." His smile faded. "I'm real sorry to hear about Mia Whitmeyer."

I swallowed, hoping my emotions wouldn't be written large on my face. "It was a tough season."

"Will she make a comeback, you think?"

"I think she's lucky to be walking. I'm not so sure about skiing."

He dropped the subject after that. A good thing, because I didn't think I could keep up the pretense.

Being back at my parents' place made me feel like I was seventeen again. I missed those days sometimes, me and my brothers joking at the table. Often as not, Mallory would come over to join us. Mallory had a family of her own now, Adam was in Utah, chasing down avalanches and Eric was a partner in the business, not a twelve year old who played too much Nintendo. And me? I was still the same old Creech, a hopeless romantic in love, once again, with the wrong woman, the one who would end up shredding my heart.

"I met her out in Park City," Eric was saying. "She lives in Creech's condo complex."

My mom passed me the ketchup. "It'll get better,

Creech. Next season, you'll do fine."

"They need to rebuild the team," my dad said.

I listened absently, my mind on something else. "Yeah. Listen, can I borrow the old truck? I want to go up to Wilmington. The house is empty, good time to do some work on it."

"I don't understand why you won't sell, son. You can't be making any money on the rental." My dad handed me a plate of fries.

"It's a soft market. Better to rent for the moment." Business was something my dad would understand. Emotional appeal, sentiment, or whatever the real reason for holding on to the place, those I could barely understand myself.

My mom, of course, read right through the soft market argument. After Eric left, my dad went out to check on the old truck. "The clutch is a little funky. I'll have a look before you take it up to Wilmington."

I helped my mother with the dishes. "Creech, you aren't holding on to the house because of Mallory, are you?" She handed me a bowl to dry. My mom loved Mallory and would have loved having her in the family.

"No, Mom. She's got Bell and Emily. I think she's pretty happy."

"I think she is, too. I'm more worried about your happiness."

I gave her a big grin. "I'm happy, see?"

She dropped a pot into the soap suds. "You don't fool me for an instant. There is something bothering you—but I won't press. I care about you. You know that, right?"

I kissed her cheek. "Of course I know. I just, well. I miss Wilmington. I know this sounds stupid, but I miss my old job. This season, it was more than just a bad year for the team."

"You lost Mia Whitmeyer." She handed me the pot and examined me for a minute. "I hadn't thought about it, how terrible her accident must have been for you. It's probably going to end her career, isn't it? And after what happened to you in Grindlewald, it's a terrible reminder."

I felt my eyes start to fill. Embarrassed, I bit my lip and concentrated on drying the pot.

"I'm sorry, honey; I didn't mean to bring up old hurts. It's just that you seem so quiet and sad. It's not like you."

It wasn't old hurts that were making me all emotional. "I'm a big boy. I'll get over it."

"If you really want to change careers, you can always come back and work here. Your father would love it, though he'd never say so. I'm serious."

"I know. I'll think about it."

Mia

After Connor and my parents left for the night, I lay back in the semi-darkness of a room that had become so familiar I could have told you how many tiles there were in the ceiling and wondered why I hadn't told Connor our break up hadn't been a mistake. I picked up Joel-bear and speculated about the man who occupied more space in my heart than my ex ever had or could. I had released Creech from any obligation to me. He owed me nothing and I had told him as much. And he'd taken me at my word. Though a big part of me wished he'd at least write and another part wondered why he hadn't.

My physical therapist, Ulrike, showed up at my bedside early the next morning. "We will try with the walking, yes?"

I was surprised they were actually letting me get out of bed. I'd been immobilized for so long I'd nearly forgotten what upright felt like. "Ready when you are."

It was much, much harder than I thought it would be. My hips ached; my legs were weak from all the time spent immobile. Ulrike showed me how to move so I wouldn't reinjure myself and it took the better part of forever just to swing my legs over the side and sit up on the bed. I had to reach out to grab the walker she'd brought and nearly fell doing it. She helped me to stand and then there I was, bent over a walker as though I were about one hundred years old, holding on to the sides for dear life.

Connor seemed to have great timing for finding me at my most vulnerable. He chose that moment to walk into the room, carrying two cups of coffee.

"Can I help?" he asked. Luckily, his hands were full; otherwise he might have grabbed me.

"We are walking slow, one time around the hall," Ulrike said.

Connor put down the coffee, sloshing some of it on Joel- bear's T-shirt, then he took hold of my shoulders. "Okay, Mia, you can do this."

Something about the way he'd said it, or maybe just having a witness at this particular moment, made my temper rise. "Let go, Connor. Could you please just get out of here?"

He looked hurt but covered it with a smile. "Sure, babe, whatever you want. I'll come back when you've finished with your therapist." He took one of the coffees and, as he left, I berated myself for being a shrew. He was just being nice, after all.

I had other things to worry about, though, like getting my legs to take steps. It took another part of forever to circle around the ward. Ulrike had to prop me up more than once along the journey.

"You do very good," she said when we were back in front of my room.

"One more time?" I asked. I was nothing if not tenacious. It's how I'd won all those damned medals and I was going to let my tenacity guide me now.

"No. Is enough. You do not want more injuries to get."

I didn't want more injuries and so I let her guide me back into the safety of my bed.

When Connor came back, I felt I had to make

amends for my outburst. "I'm sorry about earlier. I shouldn't have snapped at you like that."

"It isn't the first time you've snapped at me, Mia." His tone was teasing, but there was a hint of hurt or anger lurking under the surface. It was like our relationship, calm and inviting unless you looked down deep, where it had been troubled for a long time. Connor was good at playing the patient boyfriend, who put up with all my ambitious plans and dealt well with my competitive nature. I was good at ignoring his wants and needs in favor of my own.

"Look, Connor, if you feel the need to be here with me because of some misguided sense of guilt or responsibility or something, you can let it go. I absolve you. And maybe you'll forgive me for not putting your interests first."

He blinked, surprised as if I'd slapped him. "Jesus, Mia. We were together a long time. I've been in love with you since I was sixteen. Maybe I'm not ready to let go."

He was the one who had let go, I wanted to remind him. But I got it. "You think my accident has changed things, between us?"

"Yes, I think it has. It's made me think about what it is I want, that's all."

"I'm not sure it's me you want," I said softly.

He sighed, not answering at first. "I've got to drive back out to Reid this afternoon. I can be back in a few days. Can we at least talk this through?"

"With luck, I'll blow this pop stand in a few days."

"Then maybe we can fly home together. There will be lots of time as we cross the Atlantic."

"Okay, yes. We can share a plane and talk across the Atlantic," I said. What I didn't say was that I didn't think it would change anything. I didn't know where love went, but I did know that, as far as Connor was concerned, it had gone. And I wasn't too sure a plane ride would bring it back.

Katya Hofstadter came by to see me in the afternoon. My dad had been watching reruns of *Friends* in German, which he had decided might be a good way to pick up on the language. My mom was attempting to knit a hat. Neither enterprise was doing anything but making them frustrated, illustrated by how quickly they dropped what they were doing when Katya came in.

"Congratulations on your World Cup title," my dad said.

"Yes, thank you."

"You can also congratulate her for getting married," I added.

"How nice," my mom said.

Katya blushed, "Yes. Is very nice."

"Well," said my mom taking my father's arm. "We're going to get some coffee. You girls have a good chat."

"Maybe we can get some torte to go with the coffee," my father said.

"Ah, is a nice place for torte in two blocks, you know it?"

"We know them all," said my mom as they left.

"No joke. They've been here with me six weeks. The only good thing about it has been the torte."

"You go home soon, yes?"

"I'm hoping to be home, or at least back in New Hampshire, by the end of the week."

"I miss you at the finals, all the season. Is not the same."

"Sure, I let you win the World Cup," I grinned at her, she grinned back.

"I like this better if I beat you to win, you see?"

"Who says you would have beat me?"

She laughed and clicked her tongue, then turned serious. "You are coming back, to racing?"

That was the one question I couldn't bring myself to answer. Even now, I didn't want to consider the possibility. Though, in truth, I'd spent weeks lying flat on my back and considering. "I might make a monumental comeback, you never know."

"I think the Olympics, next year, it is my last races."

This was news. In my head Katya raced forever. More precisely, she and I raced against each other forever.

"It is hard for me, this idea to retire," she said. "Hans Jorgen and me, we talk about this and I think it will be time. We will make a family, and I will still have the skiing in my life, but it is then not so much my...alles, how do you say, all?'

I knew exactly what she meant. "I wonder if I'm ready to give up racing. I may not have a choice. I turn thirty in a few months."

"Thirty is not so old a lady. There is time for many things."

I laughed. "You sound like my mother."

"She is very smart. What does Creech say?"

"Creech?"

"He is coming to see you, yes?" She smiled and shook her head. "I am so surprised to see him in Innsbruck. Hans Jorgen and me, we come home after the last races in Zermatt. And in the morning I go to the bakery on my street and there I see Creech. I ask what he is doing there and he tell me he drives all night long from Zermatt to see you." She winked at me. "I think he is very much in love with you."

I was so astounded I didn't know what to say. After she left, I wondered why Creech would drive all night to see me and then never show up to see me.

Seventeen

Mia

I hobbled around down the corridor the next day and the day after that. I kept hoping the stiffness would go away. My body felt awkward, as though I didn't quite belong to it and this sensation was both new to me and unwanted. I had never needed to will myself to move before, not even after the most intense of workouts. It bothered me so much that, in frustration, I barked at Ulrike. "Is this ever going to get better?"

Her eyes were filled with something that looked so much like pity I had to turn away. "It will better get, yes, I think so. It must be learned again, the walking and you will remember it slowly, slowly."

What, exactly, was she trying to tell me? That I was damaged goods now? Sure, I would walk out of here but to ask for more was just plain old folly? I didn't press, reminding myself I was on my feet, which was a heck of a lot better than being flat on my back.

The day before I was to be released from the hospital in Innsbruck, I had a Facetime meeting with Mike Granberg, the head of U.S. racing. Mike was all smiles when we connected, but in his eyes was the same sort of pity I'd seen in my therapist's eyes. Was everyone going to look at me like that from now on?

"I hear you're up and walking," he said, the cheer in his voice as unconvincing as his smile.

"Yeah, I plan a long hike across the Alps. I might walk home if I can figure out the walk-on-water part." My cheer was as forced as his.

He laughed, sort of. Then allowed the frown in his eyes to meet his mouth. "I can't tell you, Mia, how sorry we are about this accident."

I nearly said something snide. I'd been six weeks in the hospital and he hadn't contacted me. "Well, shit happens."

"True. We want you back, you know that. We've got a state of the art training facility out in Park City—well, you know that, too. It's yours to use, the trainers are there for you, whatever you need. Once you're done with rehab, it's yours. Meanwhile, we've arranged a private jet to move you and your folks to Dartmouth tomorrow. You're poised to make the greatest comeback in history, and we're ready to cheer you on."

I held on to his words like a life preserver in a raging sea, I wanted to believe in them with my whole heart and soul. My body knew better. My body, with its stops and starts, wasn't the same one I'd crashed into the snow fence six weeks earlier. I was changed and my body would remind me even if I wanted to think otherwise. Still, because I wanted to believe, because I did believe in mind over matter, I said, "That sounds terrific."

He beamed at me as though I'd given the right answer. "One more thing—"

The last thing I needed was to hobble up to a podium and tell a bunch of reporters from ESPN I was doing great, but Mike could be pretty insistent and made me feel as though I owed something to the team, so I agreed to the press conference he set up in the lobby of the hospital.

"We'll be right here with you," my mom said as she wheeled me from the elevator. A few cameras flashed as Ulrike helped me from the chair and then Connor took my arm and helped me up the steps of the small stage that had been set up for the conference. My dad stood by too, looking anxious, as though he had to be ready to catch me if I stumbled. Connor kissed my cheek, which felt proprietary. I had not yet forgiven him his trespasses and wasn't at all sure I would.

I'd done press conferences before, I'd been interviewed by NBC when they covered the Olympics and after each of the games I'd been on *Late Night* and on *The Today Show*. It was kind of fun being in the spotlight, mostly because I knew my fifteen minutes were just that. A few days after my last interview, I was back to skiing and training, which was exactly where I wanted to be.

This though, this felt so much different. I wasn't here as a champion skier; I was here as someone who had taken a terrible fall and somehow managed to get up again. They wanted a hero and I wasn't one and the last thing I wanted was for the world to see me in the vulnerable state I was in. It felt as though everything in my life had become too bright and too hard. I glanced at Connor and knew he wasn't the person I wanted standing next to me as I faced this down. The person I wanted had come and left. Creech was, far as I knew, back in the States.

I thought of him as I answered the reporters' questions, of how he'd tell me I could do it, how he'd tell me I was bigger than these lights and these inquiries. "I'm here," he'd say, which was all I needed to know. I did an okay job of it, thanking the staff in Innsbruck, thanking my folks and my team for being there for me. I told the reporters I was grateful to be standing on my own two feet. What I told them was true, if somewhat sanitized. And it would have been fine, I would have come down from the platform without a scratch if one young woman hadn't asked, "What's next for you, Mia?"

I stood there, feeling as though she'd hit me with a brick instead of an innocent question. Tears welled in my eyes and I fought them back and pasted on a smile. I hoped my voice wouldn't break. "I'm not sure. Time will tell."

I turned then, and managed to step from the podium without falling on my face. I waved off the wheelchair and took one painful step and then another towards the elevator. The doors closed behind me and my small entourage, and then my whirling emotions hit me with a force I hadn't expected. I sat down in the chair and sobbed into my hands, my parents and Connor staring wordlessly down on me.

I managed to gather myself together by the time we got back to my room. My dad put his hand to my shoulder. "We'll go see about getting out of here, okay?"

I nodded and my mom asked if I needed help getting back into bed. "No, Mom, I'm going to sit for a minute, okay? Could you, maybe, go with Dad?"

She looked hurt for a second, then brightened. "Sure, honey. We'll be right back."

Connor and I watched them go as he handed me a tissue. "You're going to be fine, Mia. You are the strongest person I know."

"Connor, look—" I was ready to tell him to go home. I didn't love him anymore and he didn't love me. Why was he here? Maybe I needed to hang on to what was familiar, maybe Connor seemed a safer choice than Creech, who had driven all night and then decided it was a terrible idea. "Thanks," I said.

Creech

I stood in the great room of my farmhouse, my sleeping bag and a week's worth of clothes in a backpack at my feet, and wondered if my father had been right in saying I'd be better off selling.

Empty of furniture, the house showed its age— the windows rattled every time the wind blew, the wooden floor planks were scarred and nearly stripped of varnish, the drywall was cracked near the ceiling where water had come in during a storm. And this was just the living room; the other rooms were as bad if not worse.

Well, good, I thought, the repairs would keep me busy. I'd loaded the truck with painting supplies and tools, telling everyone I planned on spending the next few weeks doing what I could to make the place more habitable. Anyone who looked closely, though, would see this for the excuse it was. I'd come here to lick my wounds, to try and get over Mia and to decide, once and for all, what I really wanted out of my life.

I'd seen the press conference with Mia on ESPN at my folk's house. I'd watched as she teared up when asked what was next for her. My heart had gone to her and I wanted to hold her in my arms and there was Connor, backing her and telling me with his being there that she was still his. I'd felt the revelation of it clench at my stomach as Eric said something about how it would be the comeback of the century if Mia made the Olympic podium next year. He'd missed the tears in her eyes, the disillusionment broadcast there as clearly as her image, tall and sure, telling the world it was a waiting game and that she couldn't predict the future. Maybe I'd only noticed myself because I'd seen it before, in my own face cast back at me in the mirror after I tried to go back to racing after Grindlewald. Or maybe I only imagined what was there in Mia's eyes.

Mia

I would rather have flown commercial. I know how ungrateful this sounds—the private plane allowed us to fly directly from Innsbruck to Dartmouth, avoiding airport security checks and long waits at the luggage carousel, the cabin was laid out like a living room suite, with two leather couches and several armchairs, food came at regular intervals as did hot towels and pillows. It was so impressively luxurious that, when we boarded, Connor sank into one of the two couches, closed his eyes and said, "If I'm dreaming, please don't pinch me, okay?"

So there I was, confined in luxury for seven hours with three people who meant a great deal to me and shouldn't all be stuck in the same small space together for more than minutes at a time. My folks studied

Connor and then me, as though our body language would give them a clue as to what was up between us. Had they asked outright, I couldn't have given them an answer.

After the press conference, when I'd been alone in my room with Connor, after he'd told me it was going to be fine, he'd taken my face between his palms and traced his thumb over my cheek. "I still love you," he'd said quietly.

The words had made me feel guilty, because I couldn't return them. The best I could do was nod.

In the morning, as I was getting ready for discharge, my mom came in to tell me my dad was waiting in the lobby, along with Connor. "Glad to be out of here, I bet," she said as I settled into the wheelchair for a final turn down the ward.

I took a long last look at the hospital room that had been my home for what seemed a lifetime. I was more than ready to go and had I been told I needed to stay another day, another hour, I would have broken down in tears again. And yet there was a small part of me that wanted to stay, the hospital room had been a cocoon and I was about to shed it. That scared me. What if I'd forgotten how to fly? "Sooner the better," I'd said to my mom.

She went to pick up my bag and then hesitated. "Are you okay? With Connor being here?" She wasn't pushing really, and I knew if I told her everything was fine, she'd let it go.

"He's been good, I guess. Supportive."

"Good. Support is important. Does this mean—?"

"I don't know what it means." I thought again of the unanswered I love you. I thought I'd known how to read Connor, I wasn't sure I could anymore.

"He was planning to marry that girl from work," she said, gently, as though picking at the edges of a band aid that she knew would hurt like hell to yank free.

"I don't know what his plans are. He doesn't talk

about her."

"Well, he'd have to break it off, wouldn't he?"

The statement was so obvious I nearly said 'duh'. I stopped myself because I saw what she was getting at and she had a point. "I guess."

"Mia, would you want him to? Break it off?"

Part of me thought I shouldn't care one way or the other and the other part of me wanted him to break up with her, even if he and I didn't get back together, it meant somehow that I had won. And I was a winner, wasn't I? "I don't know, Mom."

So the plane cabin was filled with this unease, the unease of I don't know. I could see disapproval in my dad's eyes every time he looked at Connor. He used to love Connor, they hiked and skied together. After my brother Seb went west, he would joke that Connor was a good substitute son. When Connor broke it off with me, it was as if he'd broken up with my dad, too, and now the air was heavy with a sense of betrayal. Even if I took Connor back, I wasn't sure my dad would.

My mom, more circumspect, would make the best of it. She was good at making the best of things, so good that my dad sometimes called her 'lemonade' for her ability to deal with lemons. If Connor's coming back to me was in the works, she'd welcome him with open arms.

Connor wanted a heart-to-heart. Maybe he was as confused as I was about his feelings about us. It was impossible to have that kind of conversation with my parents there and the best he could do was cast furtive glances my way. I didn't want to have the talk with him anyway, and was happy to delay it, though I knew the delay was temporary. We wouldn't be airborne forever and at some point, I'd have to figure out what to do about him.

Eighteen

Creech

I managed to spend the first three days in Wilmington without running into anyone I knew. This was most likely because I didn't leave the house much, except to take a few long walks down the old country road I lived on. It wasn't easy to go unnoticed in a small town and sooner or later I knew someone would figure out I was here, but for the time being the solitude suited me just fine.

By day four, I started to get antsy. I knew Mallory would be upset with me for not calling and telling her I was staying a few miles from where she lived—and she'd have every right to be upset, which made me feel guilty and the longer I stayed without contacting her or Bell, the more my guilt grew. I was about ready to go to their cabin and confess when there was a knock on the door.

I'd been sanding down the windowsill in the kitchen, getting ready to re-stain it. Hours of solitude made me productive and, so far, I'd painted the living room and hallway, replaced a bedroom storm window that had been cracked and now I was setting to on the sills. I put down the sandpaper, wiped my hands on my old hole-in-the-knee jeans, and went to open the door to Mallory, who stood out on the porch looking pissed off.

"Hey, Mallo," I said, figuring for some stupid reason I could cover the unforgivable transgression of not contacting her by acting as though nothing were wrong.

"You know how I found out you were here?" Mallory folded her arms like a disapproving school teacher. "Corky Peters said she saw you at the Seven

Eleven buying coffee. I told her I was sure she was wrong." She raised an eyebrow, daring me to come up with an excuse.

I scratched my hand through my hair as though this might buy me time. "Want to come in?"

She stepped inside and frowned at the painter's tape around the doorway and crown moldings in the hall.

"I'm doing a few minor repairs," I said.

She turned the frown on me, complete with a hurt look that let me know how totally I'd messed up and betrayed our friendship.

"I was going to come see you—I was planning to soon as I finished sanding down the windowsill in the kitchen." It sounded like the lame excuse it was.

Mallory wasn't buying. She shook her head. "How long have you been here?"

I shrugged a no biggie shrug. "A couple of days."

"Jeeze, Creech."

I knew I couldn't make any more excuses. "I'm sorry, Mallo-cup. I've—it's just that I've got a lot to sort out. I didn't really want to talk to anyone." I didn't add that her and Bell's happy life with child and dog was the last thing I needed to witness with my own love life on the skids. I didn't need to be reminded of what I was missing.

"I'm not just anyone, Creech. At least I didn't used to be."

"You're not just anyone. You're right. I should have let you know." I bit the inside of my cheek and closed my eyes to keep the threat of emotion at bay. This got some sympathy.

"You really are a wreck, aren't you?"

"I'm in worse shape than my house," I admitted. "And a can of paint from Sherwin Williams isn't going to fix me."

"Come by for dinner, okay? Bell would love seeing you—and Emily, too. She talks about you. Mia Whitmeyer's coach." She stopped and frowned again.

"It's Mia, isn't it? The reason you're here?"

She'd always been really good at ferreting out my trouble, but even she didn't have that kind of ESP. Still, her question put me on the defensive. "What about Mia?"

"She was your star skier. I saw the video of her accident. It must have reminded you of Grindlewald, how could it not? That kind of thing would shake anyone up."

"It's been hard." I didn't add that being in love with Mia wasn't helping matters. Mallory had been the object of my unrequited love long enough to make a new, unreciprocated love seem like catastrophe.

"Which is another reason why you should come to dinner. Let me, let us, take care of you a little, okay?"

"I don't know if I can."

"Because you'd rather sit on the floor with a bottle of beer and takeout pizza and pick at your wounds? The Creech I know wouldn't do that. "

This pierced through my defenses. "Maybe I'm not that Creech anymore."

"If you find him, the guy who was my best friend, tell him to come over to my house for dinner. I miss him." With that she walked out the door.

Mia

Connor's cell rang the minute we deplaned. He excused himself and answered while my parents and I dealt with a small knot of reporters who had shown up at the airport. I fielded the usual questions—how long would I be in Dartmouth? What would I do afterwards?

Then I was asked if I planned to go back to skiing. "Yes. I plan on going to Park City in a month or two to work with trainers." The words were out of my mouth before I realized what I'd said, my subconscious had made up my mind for me even as I thought I wasn't sure.

My mom gave me a curious look, my dad smiled,

and Connor, who had walked back over after finishing his call, was stunned. "You are actually thinking of going back?"

"Yes. I don't know if I can race again, but having a chance to train in Park City is an opportunity I should take advantage of."

He sighed, making it clear he didn't like my answer. "Listen, I've got to rent a car and get over to Manchester. I'll be back in a few days and we can talk, okay?"

"Yes, sure. You know where I am."

He kissed my cheek. "I know where you are, for now," he said.

My parents and I arrived at Dartmouth rehab to a welcoming committee of doctors, nurses and therapists. Apparently, I was a big deal, a VIP patient, and they wanted to assure me I'd get the best treatment available. One nurse even asked for an autograph and a couple of selfies were taken with staff members.

I settled into a small dorm-like room with a hospital bed, a small desk, and a console with a TV and a dresser. Mike Granberg had arranged to get my parents' car to the center so they could drive home to Franconia. They had been away from the inn for six weeks and needed to reopen if they wanted to avoid bankruptcy, although they never would have said anything.

My mom went down to arrange the car, and once she'd gone, my dad pulled a small package from his coat. "A little coming home present," he said, handing it to me.

I unwrapped a new iPhone.

"They said you can have a phone here, and they have service, I checked. It's all set up. I even programmed in our number." He smiled like he'd just handed me the world. Maybe he had.

"Wow, Dad, you didn't have to. I know how

hard—"

He cut me off with a wave of his hand. "You are not to worry about your mom or me or the inn. We'll be fine, okay?"

I shook my head. "You've been away six weeks. That's a long time."

"We've got some set aside. And besides, you are far more important than my kitchen."

I knew that I was near a line I wouldn't and shouldn't cross. "Thanks. I promise to keep you updated on my progress."

"You are strong, Mia. I am so proud of you and what you need now is to get back on your feet and back on skis. Promise me you won't let anything or anyone stand in your way."

I knew that by anyone, he meant Connor. "I won't, Dad. I have to consider my ski racing days might be over, though."

He gave me a hug. "You listen to me, you are a champion. I doubt very much you'll ever be done skiing, it's too much a part of you."

Was I still a champion? Could I go back to the circuit and put down the kind of times that would keep me winning? Could I still race?

Creech

I went after the windowsill with vengeance after Mallory left. Just because I had feelings, because I needed some downtime, didn't mean I was a changed man. I thought she knew me, but she didn't know me at all. I finished scrubbing the finish off three of the doors and surveyed my progress. Enough for one day. I took a shower and as the water cascaded down over my head, guilt began to set in. Mallory was hurt and angry, she had every right to be. She'd been my best friend since we could both walk.

If I didn't go over to her place, it might spell the end of that friendship and I couldn't abide that. So after my shower, I put on my last clean shirt and got in my truck. I stopped and bought a bottle of wine as a peace offering.

Bell had designed and built the cabin where he and Mallory lived, a log house with a steeply pitched roof and a front porch where a pair of Adirondack chairs sat year round. It was a testament to how much Bell cared about his family. He was a soft spoken man who didn't often talk about what he was feeling. One look at the house he'd built and the furniture he'd made for his wife and child and those feelings became crystal clear, his making them was an act of love.

The cabin was in a clearing, surrounded by pine woods, with the peaks of the Adirondack Macintyre range beyond. As I drove up, the sun setting behind the mountains, I wished again that I could have something like this in my own life. I could imagine living in the farmhouse with Mia, though I was pretty sure her wishes wouldn't coincide with mine, it wasn't a house she wanted, but her career back. It wasn't me she wanted, but Connor O'Keefe.

Chance, the family dog, came bounding over as I stepped out of the truck. He barked a few times as though to warn me off, then wagged his tail and let me scratch him behind the ears. "How's it going?" I asked as the cabin's front door opened.

"Chance, come." Bell stood in the doorframe, taller than I, his blond hair pulled back into a ponytail. He saw me there and a smile played on his lips. "Creech, good to see you, man."

"Good to see you, too," I said as Chance led the way up the porch steps. "I hear you've got food."

"We do. Good thing you came by, Mallory might have gone over to your place and shot you if you hadn't."

Emily, Bell and Mallory's five-year-old daughter, came over to the door and stood next to her father, the two of them so much alike that Bell could never have denied the girl's paternity. Not that he would. He put his hand to his little girl's head. "Hey, Em, remember this guy?"

"Silly. That's Creech."

"Yup. It's me." Something in my heart lightened. It had been months since I'd seen her, though a year ago I'd been a regular part of her life. She came over and threw her arms around my middle. "We missed you, Creech." This made my heart bubble even more as I thought about my own life and wondered if Bell had any idea at all of how lucky he was.

"I've missed you, too, munchkin."

"You've been skiing with the big girls," she said as I came into the house.

Bell laughed. "She has a giant poster of Mia Whitmeyer in her bedroom. I think she likes it better than the one she has of me."

"That's not true, Daddy!" Emily turned to me. "You are Mia's coach now, right?"

I swallowed hard, it shouldn't hurt to have a simple conversation. "That's right."

"And she had an accident. Like when I did last year."

"Yeah," I said, biting the inside of my cheek again for being so foolishly emotional.

Mallory came in, her usual outfit of jeans and T-shirt, her feet bare. Mercifully, she changed the subject. Though not necessarily for the better. "You made it." Her face was deadpan, still with a hint of anger. "Good. Dinner's about ready. I made chili."

"You made chili?" I said, trying to make things lighter. It was common knowledge that Mallory was not the best of cooks.

"She's gotten pretty good at it. It's edible and everything." Bell put his arm around his wife and kissed her temple.

She elbowed him playfully. "Watch it, sweetums, if you want to eat."

Emily took my hand and pulled me towards the table. "You sit here. We setted a place for you."

"Thank you," I said. Then remembered I'd left the wine in the truck. I pointed to the door. "I brought a bottle of wine. I left it in the truck."

"Peace offering?" Mallory did know me pretty well, after all.

"You could say that." I went out to get it, wondering how I was going to get through the next few hours.

I sat in the truck's cab for a moment, just a minute, just to catch my breath because it had gotten hard to breathe. What the hell was the matter with me anyway? It was just dinner, just a simple dinner with my best friend and her family. I should be thrilled to be here.

The sun had set and the light in the windows of the cabin shone out; small pats like melting butter. How far was it to Hanover, to Mia? I could drive off and be there in a few hours time and I could tell her about the cabin with buttery light and everything I wanted and how I wanted it with her. I'd tried that already, I'd driven headlong into the realization that she didn't need me in her life, she'd be fine without me.

The door opened and shut and there was Bell, walking over towards the truck. I got out of the cab and held up the wine bottle as though it were a World Cup trophy.

"Mallory thought you'd taken off and gone to Canada or something," Bell said.

Leave it to Mallo to get close to what was in my head, though the Quebec border wasn't exactly what I had in mind. "I was just admiring the view."

Considering it was dark out, my lie sounded preposterous. Bell didn't even attempt to acknowledge it. "Mallory thought I should come out and talk to you."

"You should talk to me?" This was nearly as preposterous as admiring a view in the dark. Bell didn't say much and I'd never spoken to him about anything close to his heart. Hell, I'd barely spoken to Mallory about those things and certainly not recently.

"She's worried about you," he added. "She figures you're having some kind of weird reaction to Mia's accident. Kind of a PTSD thing, because it reminds you of your own accident. She figures it's something I'd know about." He scoffed a little. Bell, too, had suffered a bad accident a few years back. We never traded accident stories. I'm pretty sure we felt the same way about it, stuff happens and the past is the past. You can't keep licking your old wounds. If I thought about it, I was pretty sure Mia would agree with the sentiment. I would have thought Mallory understood that, too.

"So she's taken up psychology, has she? I'm not a complicated guy, pretty easy to figure out, actually."

Bell nodded. "I get that. Only, you've been holed up at your house and just now you took off as though we'd set you on fire." He smiled. "Mallo's chili really isn't that scary."

I held up the wine again. "I didn't want to leave it in the car. I should have brought beer." I figured it would be enough—he'd be satisfied and tell Mallory I was fine.

"She's not going to let it go, you know?"

"Yeah, I know. I'm fine though, really. She's right, the accident did kind of get to me—the whole season didn't turn out like I'd hoped."

"Okay," he said. "Let's go eat." I was happy he'd let it go.

The truth was, Mallory was right and if I were being honest, I'd have admitted I didn't like the pensive guy I'd become much more than she did. It wasn't me, I wasn't a guy who stared into the abyss, I was the guy who got on with things. I was fun to be with, good old likeable Creech. I could be that guy for Mallory, at least for an hour.

So I followed Bell inside and made jokes about Mallo's chili and talked about the ski season and fixing up my kitchen. I took Bell up on an offer to help me with the cabinets and listened to Emily as she talked excitedly about pee wee racing. She'd come in first in her division in slalom run at Whiteface. "She's caught the bug," Mallo said, obviously proud of her little girl.

"You're going to be a champ," I said. With a mother who'd broken an NCAA record in Giant Slalom and a father who had several extreme ski championships, it was certainly written in her bloodline.

"I'm going to be just like Mia," she said, smiling. I managed to smile back. "Want to see my posters?" She was already pulling at my arm and leading me towards her room.

Emily's room was how I pictured a typical little girl room, curtains in a rosy pink and a princess bedspread topped with a menagerie of stuffed animals. All except for the walls, which were plastered with ski posters. "I did it myself. Mommy helped," she said.

"She's a big fan," Mallo had come up behind us. "She was very insistent on what she wanted."

Over her dresser was a poster of the last Olympic women's team, and smiling down at me were Mia, Tin, Rachel, Reni and Lara with a flag and letters saying USA. "This one's my favorite." Emily climbed onto the bed and bounced over to the poster over her headboard. Mia, in a double shot—one picture of her in action, her body nearly parallel to the slope as she cut a turn through a gate, the second photo showed her beautiful face, her blonde hair around her shoulders, her sky blue eyes smiling, with the four medals she'd won in the last Olympics hung around her neck like the crown jewels. "Mia Whitmeyer," the poster read "American Champion."

I didn't think anything as simple as seeing a poster could bring me to my knees, but it nearly did. All my feelings towards Mia, towards the accident, welled up and the room nearly spun away.

"She's the best," said Emily.

"Yes, she is," I managed. Mallory must have heard the catch in my voice. She took my arm.

"Okay, munchkin, it's time for you to get into

your jammies. I'm going to dish out some ice cream." I followed Mallo back to the kitchen. "It'll get easier," she said softly.

"Will it?" I took the bowl from her.

The door shut as Bell, who had let the dog out, came back in. Mallory examined my face. "You're in love with her, with Mia." It wasn't a question.

Mia

In those early days, my first week in Hanover, I went on automatic pilot. I decided on a goal, I would ski again. I wanted to feel the speed of gliding down a hill, the snow whispering under my skis, the cold air rushing over my face. I wanted to stand at the finish and watch my name light up the top of the board. I didn't even have to tell my body how to become stronger and faster, I knew how to train, I knew how to work myself hard. And so I worked, I plowed through sweat and ache and tired. I pushed as though my life depended on it, because I honestly believed my life did depend on it. Mia Whitmeyer, ski champion, was the only woman I knew how to be.

My therapists and doctors were impressed by my efforts. They called me remarkable; they called me the miracle woman. By day five, I was walking around unaided. By day seven, I wanted to start jogging. One of my doctors, a grey-haired athletic man named Gleason, advised caution. "I know you're anxious to get back to it, but I want you to slow it down a little. I don't want you to reinjure that hip." I knew he was right and I slowed down. I didn't like it much, I didn't do low gear and it was hard to contain my intensity.

I talked to my parents each day, giving them a report of my progress. And I talked to Connor everyday with the same. The calls to Connor were short; there was a lot we didn't talk about—my feelings towards him, which were still confusing, and his towards me. We didn't talk about Lynn either and I wondered if she knew about his renewed relationship with me and how she felt about it if she did.

Connor was part of my old life and I think a part of me was sure if I could get him back, I could get everything back the way it was. And Creech? He hadn't called or written me. I knew he was probably home in upstate New York. It wasn't far and so if he had feelings for me, as Katya suggested, why didn't he come see me? The magical thinking I incorporated told me that if I hadn't slept with Creech I wouldn't have fallen on that icy slope in Innsbruck. It was a crazy way to think and the other part of me knew I was denying my feelings about him, denying I had fallen in love with him.

On my second weekend in Hanover, Connor came to see me. The rehab center had a lounge, complete with coffee and tea service and a large fireplace. I went down there under my own steam to see Connor waiting in one of the comfy chairs. His back was to me and he sat hunched forward, as though there were weights on either shoulder, rubbing his hands together, an old habit of his when he got stressed, which wasn't all that often. I stood there a minute, trying to evaluate what I was feeling. It wasn't love, though there was a sort of residual attraction—he was a good-looking guy. It was more a mix of guilt at not loving him the way I should, of not being grateful enough he'd driven out to see me, and comfort. I was comfortable with Connor, he was safe. Much safer than Creech.

I walked over to him and tapped him on the shoulder and he jumped up and gave me a hug. "Wow," he said, looking me over. "One week and look at you bouncing in here."

"Thanks." I sat down on the chair next to his. "This place has a lot to recommend it. Restaurant style dining, day and night room service. I might want to stay forever."

"Yeah. I doubt that." He took my hand. "You never were one to stay put for too long."

It was a barb, the old argument that had pried us

apart in the first place—Mia doesn't want to settle down and Connor does. I wondered if it was intentional, or just a reflex action, words spoken out of turn. I decided to let it go. "Well, if the doctors are right, I'll be out of here in two weeks."

Connor let go of my hands. "That soon, huh? And then they stamp you healthy and let you go?"

"Yup. Good as new. Though it's going to take a lot of training to make the team again. We're not talking just good enough, you know?"

He stared at me, a hurt look crossed his eyes. "So you're going to Park City. For sure?"

"That is the plan. As I told you, I owe it to myself to see if I can get back what I've lost."

Connor didn't say anything for a minute, then got up. "They have espresso, I noticed. Want one?"

"No thanks." I followed him to the coffee set up and watched him make an espresso. He would douse it with cream and add some sugar. One cube. I knew a lot about him.

"You want to talk about it?"

"There isn't anything to talk about is there, Mia?"

I wanted to remind him he'd been the one who waltzed back into my life, who had said "I still love you." I was the one he'd left behind. "I'm getting better, doing better than expected. I thought you'd be happy for me."

"Of course you're doing better than expected. You always were the best, right? Only I'd think being the best gets lonely."

I wanted to rip the stupid cup from his hands and throw it across the room. Not my style, though. "This is my life, Connor. Can you please understand that? I can't just let it go."

A sadness crept into his eyes and then he looked away, to the manicured lawn outside the window. "I keep thinking, no hoping, we still have a chance. Things are different now."

"They are different. You left me for someone else."

"I would never have done that if you had," he

swallowed hard, "if you had cared even a little bit about anything except your career."

"Oh, so you love me, but only if I'm the person you want me to be?" I bit out the words, angry now at his audacity.

"I love you anyway. I left Lynn."

That little piece of information pierced me. I didn't know what to make of it. "Okay."

"Not okay. Not okay at all." He plunked the sugar cube into his cup and stirred. "You asked me before what I wanted. The short answer is you."

"But?" I waited for the other part. I could have predicted what it was.

"You know the but part, Mia. You have to meet me halfway."

"And what is halfway, Connor?"

"You start to think about the future. The real future, not just your next season, your standings in the Cup, the next Olympics. You think beyond that and let me know how, or if, I fit in."

How could he ask me to give up my life? He had been a part of my life, he'd had my love, and he'd tossed it aside. "You're going to have to give me some time."

"You've had time, Mia. Years and years worth."

"Don't. Please. That's not what I meant." I felt tears start to well. I chased them away.

He traced his finger over my cheek. "Okay, fine. Take some time. Let me know what you want. If you go to Park City, though—I don't think I can wait that long."

I stepped back from his hand. "So, Park City or you?" I couldn't believe he'd given me an ultimatum. I couldn't believe I'd consider giving in to it.

"I'm trying to be honest here. I've given up something."

"I can't—"

He took my hands. "You can think about it. I get that you have to think about it. Just don't think too long."

"Fair enough."

"Fair enough." He kissed me, a soft and tender kiss, warm and comforting, tasting slightly of strong coffee and sugar. I closed my eyes and kissed him back, hoping to find the spark, the intensity I'd felt when Creech kissed me. I couldn't.

Creech

Bell came over to the farmhouse and together we sanded down the kitchen cabinets and began staining them. We talked about skiing and sports in general. We talked about his extremes business, where he guided skiers through back woods and off-trails skiing. He wasn't taking the big risks anymore. "You miss it?" I asked.

He paused for a moment, the sandpaper clenched between his fingers. "I'm thirty-one years old, I have a wife and a little girl. Maybe there comes a time when you have to re-examine your priorities."

"Yeah. I get that. You're a lucky man. I'd trade places with you."

"You can't have Mallory," he deadpanned.

"I know. You won her over fair and square. She loves you, man."

"I believe she does." He broke into a smile. "Mallo is the best thing ever happened to me."

"For the record, she never would have cheated on you with me."

"Why do you think I trust you with her? Besides, she's pretty sure you're into Mia Whitmeyer."

I groaned. "She told you that?"

He went back to carefully sanding the small groove in the cabinet door. "Women love a good romance. You wouldn't think it, but Mallo's no exception."

"Yeah, well. She might be right."

"That's great, Mia's perfect for you."

"She's not. My feelings for her don't make for a great coach/athlete relationship. Mallo's right about

Mia's fall, too. It did freak me out."

"It was an accident. No one can stop an accident. You and I, we both know that firsthand." He stirred the can of wood stain he'd opened. "There are so many things I should have said to Mallory early on. I regret I didn't tell her how much I loved her, right from the start. It's worked out for me, which is just plain luck. I could have avoided a lot of pain, though. I'm just saying."

"Trouble is, I'm not sure how Mia feels about me."

"Maybe you ought to find out."

Mia

After Connor left, I went back to my room, lay on my bed and stared at the ceiling. I felt like I was standing at a busy intersection and any way I decided to cross would end up with me run over. Absently, I picked up Joel-bear. He'd been one of the first things I'd unpacked when I got here. That should have told me something. "What am I going to do?" I asked him.

He answered me. Not in words, of course, but I was holding onto the bear for a reason. He was my connection to Creech. I could decide to retire, marry Connor and go on from there. Or I could try to get back onto the circuit, with Creech as my coach, have a working relationship but not a personal one. So maybe I'd have to give up on the idea of Creech either way. Our relationship was ill fated. It always had been. But the thought of giving it up, of never seeing him again, hurt more than I thought possible.

Nineteen

Creech

I kept thinking over what Bell had said. It was the first time he'd ever given me advice on anything except maybe how to sand my floors. A cafe on Main Street in Lake Placid had a hot spot, and so I went there and checked my messages. I think I was afraid someone from U.S. Skiing would tell me not to bother to come back. I'd made a mess of the season. I'd crossed a line when I slept with Mia, too. Though I would do it again if the opportunity presented itself.

I guess I was also hoping there would be some kind of message from her, though I knew I was kidding myself. I scrolled through—there had been a few calls, from my brother, from Mike Granberg at U.S. Ski. None from Mia. Her silence told me everything I needed and didn't want to know.

I called Mike. There was no way I could figure out anything unless I knew if I still had a job.

"You're a hard guy to track down," he said.

"Yeah, sorry about that. I have this farmhouse up in the Adirondacks and it's off the grid. No Wi-fi, no cell phone service." It was more information than Mike needed and I wondered why I felt the need to excuse myself in such detail.

"I'm glad you checked in. I'd like to meet up with you in person. Can you be in Park City next Tuesday?"

I told him I'd be there. After I got off the phone, I turned the conversation over in my head, trying to analyze it for clues. He wanted to meet, why? Was he going to fire me? I knew him well enough to know that if I was going to be called to account for my season, I was going have to do it face-to-face. I dreaded going out to Park City.

I called my brother and told him I'd meet him in Wells and asked if he could give me a ride down to the airport. If I was going to Park City, I might as well get there sooner rather than later. That conversation got me wondering in a new direction. Was there room for me at the family ski area? Was working with Eric and my dad and Harry Prescott something I'd want? I hadn't been entirely kidding when I told Bell I'd trade places with him. I could see myself in a quieter life, without the constant travel, with a house and a wife and some kids and a dog. I amended the thought—with Mia. Though I was sure Mia wouldn't see herself in the rosy imaginary life I painted.

Mia

I spent the next few days in a funk. My body was on autopilot, it had been well-tuned for so long and was so used to a training regimen that it kept propelling me towards my goal even as my mind was elsewhere.

More than once I thought about calling Creech, or at least messaging him to ask him why he'd walked away in Innsbruck and why he'd given Katya the impression he loved me. His silence gave me the only answer I needed. He'd walked away because he'd come to his senses. He realized what a fool he'd been for trying to love me. As much a fool as Connor. No, worse, because his entanglement with me would mean gambling his job.

I didn't call Connor either. Though the longer I thought about it, the more I knew what my answer to his ultimatum would be. He finally called to say he wanted to see me before I left Dartmouth, which would be within a week's time.

He came up to my room carrying a bouquet. "You've always loved tulips," he said, handing them to me before kissing me with more conviction than I could return. Then he stepped back and looked me over. His smile faded. I guess I knew it would—we'd been together long enough for him to be fluent in my body language.

"You're going to Park City," he said, an accusation in his tone.

My heart hurt. I didn't want to hurt him. I didn't want to hurt either of us. I nodded. "I'm sorry. You were right to leave me. I'm not—I can't give you the kind of relationship you deserve."

He sat down on the edge of my bed and raked his hands though his hair, looking so forlorn I nearly told him never mind. I'd stay for him.

"Answer me this, Mia. Did you ever love me?"

"Of course I did." All the good times we'd had together raced through my brain—Connor holding my hand as we watched fireworks, Connor sitting behind me on a toboggan, his arms around my waist as we careened down the hill behind the inn. Connor undressing me for the first time, his eyes heavy with want. I had loved him. Hadn't I?

"I don't believe you ever did." He stood up and walked out the door without looking back.

No, I wanted to shout. I did love you. It's just that I loved skiing more.

"You're not coming home?" My mom sounded disappointed.

"I'm ready to go back," I answered.

My parents had come to Hanover to see me the day before I was to be released. They sprang me from the rehab center so we could have dinner at a little bistro downtown. The chef owner was a friend of theirs and he gave us a quiet table in the back and a complimentary bottle of wine.

"You're sure this is what you want?" my mom asked once we'd ordered.

"Of course it's what she wants," my dad answered for me.

I took a sip of wine. The truth was, I didn't quite know what I wanted, I knew what I had to do. Or thought I did, anyway. "It's a great opportunity. The facilities in Park City are fabulous. The trainers are top notch. I have to go."

"You do have choices." My mom frowned at me. "My God, Mia. Six weeks ago we weren't sure you'd ever walk again."

"That's just the point," I said. "I can walk. I can better than walk. Even after what happened. Shouldn't I see what else I can do?"

"Damn straight, you should." My dad raised his glass to me.

My mom turned her frown on him. "What does Connor say?"

The conversation I'd had with Connor felt like a bruise on my heart. Maybe it was a necessary bruise, but it would still need time to heal. "We're done."

"He broke it off?" My dad's hand tightened around the stem of his glass.

I put my hand on his. "No, Dad. I broke it off. Connor and I aren't right for one another. I think I've known for a long time. I think he probably has, too."

"Well, then, that's done." My mom smiled wistfully. "I guess my dreams of planning a wedding for you won't come true anytime soon." She took my other hand. "But then, you're no ordinary daughter. I got to see you win a gold medal. More than once. That's not something every mom can say."

"You might just get to see her win another one." My dad's smile was broad. I didn't want to disappoint him.

Creech

I hadn't lived in my Park City condo long enough for it to feel like home. I wondered if it ever would feel that way, the way my farmhouse still did, as I unpacked my clothes and filled up the refrigerator. I would meet with Mike in the morning and, tired from my flight, I went to bed early and slept uneasily, again rehashing the conversation we'd had on the phone.

Mike hadn't sounded particularly reassuring; then again he hadn't sounded particularly anything. I wanted to trust Davy Delacroix, but I wasn't sure he wouldn't make a play for my job. He wasn't, from what I'd learned working with him, a vindictive guy. Still, he might have told Mike about my relationship, or the rumors of my relationship with Mia, out of a sense of responsibility to the team.

By morning, I'd decided I would come clean about what had happened with Mia. Mike would find out about it sooner or later—and better he heard it from me than from someone else.

I met Mike at his office in the training center. It was just down the hall from my own cramped office, though the only other time I'd stepped inside it was when Mike had called me in to tag me for the job as head coach. It had been a big step up, and I was kind of surprised I'd been selected. Though I'd been coaching with some success at the developmental levels, there were lots of others with similar experience.

"You're young, you've got a lot of energy, and you have a spectacular record as a development coach," Mike had reassured me then. "And you've been a racer at these levels, you know what it takes," he'd added as though he needed to sell me on the job.

I didn't think he'd be assuring me now. A year later and the gamble he'd taken on me hadn't paid off. It sure hadn't turned out the way I'd hoped it would. Mike met me at the door, his coat still on. "What say we get some coffee?"

"Sure." I wished I knew how to read his invitation and then decided I needed to stop trying to read into everything.

"There's this great little coffee shop down the street, do you know it? They roast their own beans. Best dark roast Jamaican I've ever had the pleasure of drinking."

We went down to the cafe, in the heart of the tourist area, got our coffee and sat down, me again analyzing why he'd want to talk here. I could have come up with a good reason, it was less formal, he really did love the coffee here, but all I could think about was several women I'd broken it off with—how each time, I'd chosen a public place to do it.

I took a sip and set the cup down. I figured there was no point in beating around the bush. I might as tell him everything. If he didn't know, then he would find out sooner or later anyway. "Full disclosure. Yes, I had an affair with Mia Whitmeyer and no, I don't regret it. And yes, we had a crappy season, which is on my head. I do regret that."

A smile crept over Mike's craggy face. "That kind of straight forwardness is one of the main reasons I hired you for the job."

I swallowed away my fear. "And now you're going to fire me."

"What would make you think that?"

I'd already given him the reasons. "Davy might be better suited to the job than I am."

Mike took a sip of coffee. "God, that is good coffee." Then he looked me hard in the eye. "You think I didn't consider Davy for the job? Don't get me wrong, I like the guy, but he hasn't got the rapport with the team you do. You can connect with the girls, because you care about them and you like to win as much as they do. Which is why you're beating yourself up over a season when a lot of what happened was not your fault."

I waited for the rest to come. As a coach, I'd always couched the bad news between the layers like a sandwich, the theory being it was easier to take. The rest came soon enough. "I wonder, though, if you'd want me to fire you so you don't have to quit."

I was taken aback. I wasn't a quitter. Even when I'd left my racing career, all those years ago, it had been to pursue something I wanted more. I was a terrible poker player; I couldn't bluff to save my life. Mike read me easily and so I said what was on my mind. "Truth? Most days I feel like I'm in over my head. It's a big job. The racers, they're tough. Grown up and different from the girls at the development level."

"Yes, they are. And when they fall, they fall awful hard." He gave me a pointed look.

The thought that Mallo had been telling me the same thing crossed my mind. How torn up was I? Did it show that much?

"Look, Creech," Mike continued. "Everybody feels terrible about what happened to Mia, me included. You, though, from what I gather, it's hit you harder than most and set you spinning. And if you can't handle it, I need to know."

"I can handle it," I said, maybe a little too stridently. He'd hit a nerve. "It's just that I—"

"You have feelings for Mia that extend beyond the usual coach/racer relationship."

"They extend beyond friendship."

"That could be difficult. If she comes back."

"I haven't seen her in a while, so there's nothing between us anymore."

"You might want to keep it that way."

Mike's message was loud and clear. I was going to have to make a choice between Mia and my job. Though since Mia had taken up with her old boyfriend, she'd pretty much made the choice for me. The other question was could I be 'just friends' with Mia? We'd tried just friends before and it hadn't worked out too well.

Mia

I went to Park City with high hopes. Everyone kept telling me how exceptional I was and, under most circumstances I would have ignored those comments as just a way to get my head out of the game. Things had changed and now I clung to those compliments because I needed them, I wanted badly to believe everything ever written about me as superwoman was true.

Things were different. The changes were subtle, not readily apparent, but I felt them down in my bones. The first day, I planned a short training session in the training pool. The pool, a sort of treadmill for swimmers, supported the weight bearing tendons and muscles still healing and was a great place to build stamina. Swimming wasn't my favorite sport and I wouldn't count myself as a great swimmer, but I was proficient enough to rack up a few miles worth of exercise. My body responded well for the first mile and then the tired set in, a deep tired I had trouble fighting. I managed a second mile, which should have pleased me, but as I got out of the pool I wasn't energized, the way I usually was after a workout, and a vague question kept finding its way into my brain. Why exactly are you doing this? It was a question I'd never needed to ask before. I chased it away, not wanting to know the answer.

I dried off and got into my street clothes. And then, as I was leaving, I saw Creech getting into his truck. He didn't see me, which was a good thing. Everyone was on hiatus so I hadn't expected he'd be here. His presence shook me more than it should have.

As I drove myself home, a large part of me wanted to go over to Creech's condo and ask him what the hell he thought he was about by not calling me, by showing up and leaving the way he did in Innsbruck. The fantasy was he'd say he loved me too much and we'd fall into each other's arms. The more rational part of me thought avoiding him was a very good idea. Rationality won out, but the experience, both Creech and the training pool, left me feeling uneasy. I needed to talk to someone. I called Tin.

I'd spoken to Tin every week or so since I'd come home from Innsbruck. She did most of the talking, nine months pregnant, restless and uncomfortable, it was good for me to listen to her life. That way I wouldn't have to listen to my own.

"How's my God daughter?" I asked, glad to have

her on the line to distract me from my thoughts.

"Sitting on my bladder. I have to pee every ten minutes."

"Poor you."

"How's Park City?"

"Okay."

"Really? Okay? That's all you've got to report? "

Tin was the one person who might get what I was going through and there I was avoiding her. "It's hard." I started to cry. It came on suddenly, like a thunderstorm in summer, big hot tears that took me by surprise.

"Mia?"

I realized I'd been sobbing into the phone. "Yeah. I'm still here. I'll be fine."

"You don't sound fine." The alarm in Tin's voice was palpable. I was Ice, tough and smooth. I didn't do crying.

"Sorry, I don't know what's come over me."

"Okay, listen to me. You are going to repack your suitcase and get the first flight out to Boulder." When I didn't answer, she added "If you aren't knocking at my door by tomorrow, I'll come get you. Trust me, you do not want a hugely pregnant woman chasing you down."

"Thanks for the offer, Tin. I can't. I've—I need to train. It's going to take time."

"You need to get your head straight, girl. Come to Boulder."

I nearly told her no again, but I needed Tin more and training could wait a week or two. As an added bonus, I could avoid seeing Creech for a while. "Okay, I'll see you tomorrow," I said.

Twenty

Mia

Tin's smile as she opened the door nearly made me break down all over again. "You look good," I said, as she hugged me against her huge belly.

"I look enormous. Jack thinks it's great. I think he's nuts."

I got settled into my room and Tin made us both some tea. "I can't drink coffee. There's a whole list of things I can't do." She got out a packet of Oreos. "I can eat these, though." She took one, pulled it apart and licked the middle.

"Those are on my shall-not list. I've put on five pounds," I said.

She cocked her head and examined me. "You look terrific. It's a miracle—you look as fit as you did before your accident."

"I'm not the same, though. There's the trouble."

The kettle whistled and she poured hot water over tea bags in two mugs. "Well, hell, you've got every trainer in Park City lined up to help you out. And I know you—you're downright scary when you get to work."

"Yeah, well, skiing was my life." Was—past tense—slipped out of my mouth. It surprised me, even shocked me a little.

Tin noticed the slip, she gave me a curious look. "And now?"

"I don't know. I can't step away. Connor asked me to and I couldn't."

"Maybe you couldn't because you don't want to spend your life with Connor."

True enough, I thought. Mostly because it

wouldn't be fair to Connor to be involved with a woman whose mind kept flipping over a night with another man. It would be a kind of constant cheating. I'd told Tin all about Connor's return, but I hadn't told her about Creech. "I did something stupid."

"I don't think breaking it off with Connor was stupid, Mia. Not from what you've told me anyway."

"No, not that." And I told her about my affair with Creech.

"So you slept with him, big deal."

"It is a big deal. He's the coach. And don't give me the 'Katya married her coach' line. Hans Jorgen is her private coach, not team coach."

"It was one night. You haven't seen him since when?"

"Since the hospital in Innsbruck. No, not true. I saw him in Park City yesterday. He didn't see me." I took a sip of my tea and closed my eyes, conjuring the sight of him again. "Maybe I should have gone up to him. Maybe..."

"You don't owe him anything," Tin said. I didn't know how to answer. She took a sip of her tea. "Unless—are you in love with him?"

"One night does not a love affair make," I said, maybe a little too stridently.

"Are you trying to convince me or yourself?"

"I was with Connor forever. I broke it off because I wanted to get back to skiing. And so now I'm having second thoughts about skiing because of Creech? That doesn't make sense."

"I didn't say you were having second thoughts because of Creech. You just did."

I was ready to give her a million and one reasons why she was wrong. My rethinking my priorities had nothing to do with Creech. It was my age, my body, a change of heart I hadn't counted on.

"Holy shit." Tin put her hand to her belly and grimaced.

"Tin, are you okay?"

"I think I just had a contraction. I'm not due for another two weeks."

"What do you need me to do?" I felt calm, ready, the little voice in my head telling me I could handle this. I hadn't heard that little voice since the last time I stood in the start house before a race.

"They're gone. Probably Braxton Hicks contractions. They're kind of a warm up for the real thing." She looked up at me. "That's probably it."

A few minutes later she was doubled over again.

"I think it's the real thing, Tin."

"They said if they're less than five minutes apart, I should go to the hospital. I think that was less than five minutes."

"Get your jacket, you're going to have yourself a baby," I said.

"I'm not even packed. They said have a suitcase ready, but I haven't packed yet." She sounded as if this was a terrible flaw in her character. It wasn't like her at all, then again she'd never been in labor before.

"I'll pack up. Nightgown, underwear, and change of clothes, right? You call Jack and your doctor." I went to her bedroom and rooted through her dresser for clean clothes, which I threw into the suitcase without bothering to refold. She was at the door when I came down. "I don't know what I would do," she said, before doubling over again.

I helped her into the car and strapped her seatbelt around her. "Oh shit," she said. "My water just broke. You're going to have some explaining to do to the Avis people."

"Let me worry about that," I said, backing from the driveway. I stepped on the gas and drove like a demon as Tin barked out directions in between groans and curses.

"You are such a speed freak," she said as we pulled up to the emergency entrance.

"Fast is my thing," I grinned at her as I got out of the driver's seat, car still running, to help her out of the passenger side.

"You can't park here." A security guard came running over while pointing to the 'no parking or standing' sign directly next to the car. Tin had managed to extricate herself from the car and the security guy took one look and then took her arm. "I'll get her inside. You can park over there." He pointed to a spot where the sun glimmered off the hoods and roofs of cars in the distance.

It would take me a while to drive, park, and return. I wasn't about to leave Tinny to strangers. "Can't I just go in with her?"

Before he could argue, Tin said, "Go park and hurry back, okay? You're not the only one good at fast."

I parked the car, grabbed Tin's overnight bag, and sprinted the distance back to the hospital, my hip shouting at me to slow down. I didn't slow until I got to the emergency entrance. There was no one at emergency admittance. I figured they'd brought her up to maternity, so I ran to the elevators, looked up the floor and took the stairs, not wanting to wait. My hip hurt and I couldn't run down the long corridor to the maternity ward, so I sort of fast walked and limped to the double doors, opened them, and nearly ran Jack over on the other side.

He caught my arm. "You got here quick," I said.

"Yeah, I work down the street." He had this big goofy grin on his face. "I can't believe this." Then the smile faded. "What the hell is wrong with me? I need to find Tin."

I followed him to the nurse's station. "My wife? Christina Wilder?" I was funny to hear him call her by her married name, as though Christina Wilder were another whole person who'd replaced Tin Reardon.

"Yes, Mr. Wilder. Come with me." She stopped to look me over.

"She's with me." Jack put his hand to my arm. "Tin—Christina—would want her with us."

Tin was in bed in one of the birthing rooms. In

the short time since I'd dropped her off, she'd changed into a hospital gown, been put to bed and hooked to a monitor. Jack nearly ran to her side and took her hand and kissed her hard as I sat in a chair at the edge of the room because my back had started hurting, too.

Luckily, neither Jack nor Tin noticed. "How are you doing?" Jack asked her.

"Hurts like hell. Remind me never to sleep with you again."

The goofy grin returned. "We're really doing this thing."

A nurse came in and looked us over. "You the coach?" she asked Jack.

"Yup. I'm ready."

"That's good, cause I'm not," said Tin.

I got up and forced myself to walk straight over to the bed. The pain had subsided and I found I could ignore it. "And you are?" the nurse asked.

"She's the assistant coach," Tin said before letting out a yowl that could scare small animals in a nine-mile radius.

Jack went pale as the nurse pulled on gloves and said, "Let's have a look." She examined Tin and then looked up and smiled. "You are fully dilated. It won't be long now."

"Already?" Jack's voice had gone up an octave.

"Sooner is better," Tin said. Jack was on one side of the bed and I was on the other. Tin squeezed both our hands and if her grip on mine was any indication, it would take us both a week to get feeling back.

If there was a record for fastest birth, Tin might have broken it. Anna Mia Wilder, seven pounds and four ounces, was born one hour after we'd arrived at the hospital. I didn't have much experience with babies and the thing that struck me was how tiny she was, and how vividly alive as she cried and open and shut her miniature fingers. They washed her and swaddled her and then handed her, squalling, to Jack. He held her in his arms as though she were the best gift he'd ever received and she quieted and fell asleep. He handed her back to Tin and I snapped a picture of the three of them with my phone, capturing how both new parents were lit up like Christmas trees, elated wouldn't begin to describe it. A mix of things roiled through my gut, happiness for Tin and Jack, amazement at the tiny human they'd made together, and a kind of sadness, like I was outside with my nose pressed to the glass wishing for what was inside the window.

Creech

Adam called the day after my meeting with Mike to ask if I wanted to do some backpacking in the Wasatch Mountains. There was a hike into a place called Timp Basin, about ten miles in through some great scenery. It was a welcome diversion from my muddled thoughts and I jumped at the chance to leave Park City behind me for a few days.

I'd done a lot of backpacking and hiking through the Adirondacks back home—over the years I'd become a member of the forty-sixers, hikers who had climbed all forty-six peaks over four thousand feet in New York State. The terrain was often rough and the woods were wild, dense with pines and thick stands of maple and birch. The west was an entirely different place, the trees were spare, the terrain steep and rocky, and the land wide open. The mountains were tall outcroppings that dwarfed anything below them. The air at the higher altitudes was thin and it seemed like we were a whole lot closer to the sky. It was spectacular, but I kept comparing it to the trails at home and thoughts of them made me nostalgic and homesick. I wondered if I'd ever think of Utah as home.

We hiked into the basin and set up camp, setting our sleeping bags out under the broad sky, we figured we'd sleep under the stars like the cowboys of old. Instead of beans we ate freeze-dried beef stew and the coffee was instant. Still, it tasted good after a long day's hike and as the exertion of climbing through these mountains settled into my bones I felt more relaxed than I had since I moved to Park City.

"Eric told me you're thinking of selling the farmhouse," Adam said as we sipped our coffee from tin cups.

"Dad thinks I should. I'm still not sure what I want to do."

"Why? It's a long commute from Park City—and you spend most of your life on the road." His remark reminded me of what Mia said long ago. I'd told her I wanted to hold on to a piece of my past. Maybe I still did. The truth of the matter was that a four-bedroom farmhouse suited me better than a condo I only visited between trips and a life spent moving from hotel to hotel, ski area to ski area.

"It would be a great place to raise a family," I said of the farmhouse.

Adam raised his cup. "Something you not telling me?"

"No. I'm just saying." I thought of Mia, the house, a future different from the one I'd carved out for myself.

Adam sipped his coffee. "Well, I might just be in need of a house." He twirled his cup between his fingers and smiled softly. "I've met someone. It might be the real thing."

My brother, the guy who had dated more women than I ever would, probably in numbers adding up to the population of a small city, had finally fallen in love. "Well, that's something," I said.

"Yes. It is. Her name's Jenna and she's—amazing. She's having dinner with us when we get back tomorrow, so you can meet her then."

"So, I'm like the family rep? I get to decide if she's worthy of the Crèches' clan?" I couldn't help teasing him.

He smirked at me. "You just wait. Someday a great woman is going to turn you upside down. It's not so bad, by the way. How is your love life, anyway?"

"Non-existent."

"Come on, man. You travel around with a bus load of hot women." His smile faded. "Shit, I'm sorry. I know Mia Whitmeyer is kind of a touchy spot for you. What happened to her is damn awful."

Were my feelings for Mia really that obvious? Then again, the accident was awful. "She's coming back—she's in Park City."

"No kidding? That's awesome. That would be something, wouldn't it? Her taking a medal next year?"

"Yup. It's a story made for a fucking Disney Movie."

Adam frowned at me, I'm pretty sure he was wondering where the outburst had come from. "Something wrong, Creech?"

"No." I got up. "If I know you, you're going to insist we break camp at dawn's first light, so I think I better turn in."

We didn't talk much on the hike out. Quiet wasn't my usual mode, but Adam didn't seem to notice. Out of sorts, I wasn't ready to talk about it to Adam or anyone. Problem was, I couldn't quite figure why I'd felt so angry. It wasn't Adam, his remark about Mia's comeback was innocent enough and not different from what anyone else might say. So why did Mia's comeback attempt make me want to punch a wall?

Mia

Tin was discharged a few days after Anna Mia was born. It was a big transition for her and Jack both, a momentous thing to become parents, and I got caught up in the moment. Whenever I held the baby, I felt this shift, as though the stars were trying to realign.

Tin's mom and dad came to stay with her. Jack's parents and sister and several aunts and uncles came to visit, crowding the house with gifts and advice. After three days, I knew I'd stayed long enough and I told Tin I was going to go back to Park City. "You know, the thing about three days, fish and guests start to stink, or however it goes."

Tin had just finished nursing the baby. "You're not a guest. You get to stay as long as you want." She seemed to mean it, but I knew I had to get on with my life and let her get on with hers.

Anna started to fuss and Tin looked tired enough to sleep standing up. "Here, I'll walk her around for a while," I offered.

"See, that's why you can stay. You can be our nanny. Nanny Mia." Tin rocked in the chair as I walked the baby around, jiggling her over my shoulder. Anna let out a belch and then fell asleep, her warm little face snuggled against my neck. "You're the baby whisperer," Tin said.

"I think she was ready to drop off anyway." I could have put her down, but I didn't. I liked the small, solid weight of her in my arms.

"You can get yourself one of these, you know," Tin said.

"Not in the cards. It is my destiny to get back on my skis and be a world beater." I could taste the bitterness in the thought. I hoped it wouldn't be noticeable. I should have known better.

"Bullshit. You're ready to move on, Mia. You just can't let yourself." She got up out of the chair and put her hand on her daughter's head. "Sorry, that was harsh. You already are a champion, Mia. No one can ever take that away from you. I know you don't want to hear this, but maybe you ought to go to Creech Crèches and tell him how you feel about him."

"God, Tin. I'm not going to be the one who sets a wrecking ball to his career. He doesn't deserve that."

"You don't have to be the reason. You could quit, there are millions of opportunities for you. You and I both know it." She took the baby from me. "I think you'd like to be with Creech and you are sacrificing something that could be perfect for you for something that isn't working for you anymore."

Creech

I'd never seen Adam iron anything in his life, but the night before our dinner out with his new girlfriend, he dug a steam iron from the back of the linen closet, spread a beach towel on the dining room table, and went after his shirt with a vengeance. Since I hadn't planned on dinner out, he loaned me a shirt as well, and a pair of khakis.

"You want to do this one, too?" I asked, holding the blue oxford out to him.

He raised the iron like a gun. "Don't tempt me," and pushed a button to make steam hiss from it.

I had been petulant on the hike back and I could almost hear Mallory asking what had happened to old Creech, and who was the surly guy who'd replaced him? Feeling apologetic, I decided now was as good a time as any to clear the air. "Look, Adam, about yesterday. I'm sorry I haven't been better company."

Adam ironed the collar with the iron tip. "You've been worse. I figure long as neither of us is bloodied or bruised, we're doing okay."

"Really? We haven't always gotten along, but..."

He scoffed. "You might not believe this, but I care about you. Whatever it is, you'll figure it out, right?"

"Right."

So there I was, dressed in my brother's shirt and pants, sitting at the bar of a steakhouse, waiting for the love of his life to walk in and remind me the love of mine wasn't in my life at all. We both ordered beers and Adam sat watching the door, his fingers ticking on the beer glass.

She was pretty, was Jenna, a girl with chestnut hair falling over her shoulders and intensely brown eyes. Adam couldn't keep his own eyes from her and I had the feeling I'd disappeared from the room. It was a feeling I knew well, other people tended to blend into the background for me every time Mia entered a room. I could see her in my mind's eye, those impossibly long legs, those sapphire eyes, her entire being a statement of power and grace and beauty. Her absence was a black hole. I wanted her here. I wanted her with me.

Adam made introductions and the three of us got a table. I could see how Adam touched his knee to Jenna's under the cloth, how he reached for her at every possible opportunity. And me, the third party, sitting by, making conversation about the weather and skiing and life on the road.

That night, cocooned in my sleeping bag on Adam's couch, I felt like I'd been alone too long. I didn't want to be alone anymore. I didn't want to walk away from Mia. Not without a fight.

Twenty One

I called Eric when I got back to Park City. Tossing and turning with the springs of Adam's couch sticking into my back gave me time to think about my future and when I thought about it, whatever it was I was headed towards—a career as head coach—left me feeling empty. I didn't give my younger brother time for small talk. "How would you feel about my coming back to Wells?" I asked soon as I got him on the line.

There was a pause and I knew I'd caught him by surprise. Hell, I'd caught myself by surprise. "You serious?"

"Dead serious. I've done a lot of soul searching over the past few weeks. Something in my life isn't working and I need to change it."

"And taking a giant step backwards to here helps you how?"

His attitude wasn't what I expected and it was my turn to be silent for a minute. "Look, if you don't need me to horn in on your running of the place, just tell me."

"No. Hell, no. I could use the help and you have a share in the area, whether you work here or not. But, wow. I guess I just don't get it. It's—it's nothing like ski racing. No traveling around, no glamorous resorts, no pretty girls—well, not a lot of them anyway."

"That's exactly the point," I said.

* * *

I bought two Jamaican roast coffees at the shop Mike Granberg liked and hiked over to his office. "What can I do for you?" he asked as I handed him one of the cups.

"I thought about what you said."

"I say a lot of things." He took a sip. "Can you be

more specific?"

"About how I was hoping you'd fire me."

He put the cup down. "I didn't actually say that, did I? I don't think I made a mistake in bringing you up here."

"I think it was a mistake for me. I'm handing in my resignation. I think there are about eight guys after my job, you can have your pick."

Mike stared at me. "I guess I shouldn't, but you want to tell me why? And please don't tell me it's Mia Whitmeyer."

"It's not Mia. Not directly, anyway. I'm just—the job isn't me. I was happy in development, I thought I'd be even happier here. But I'm not."

"And this has nothing to do with Mia's accident?"

"Only in that it kind of clarified things for me." I figured I might as well lay everything down. "She's not going to come back, you know." This was something I'd been thinking for a long time. She needed to figure it out for herself, but the odds were stacked against her big time, despite who she'd been.

Mike surprised me. "Yeah, I know her chances are slim to none. I think we're all buying into a fairy tale, but it would make a hell of a story if she pulled it off."

Mia

Me, of all people, a woman who made a living as an athlete, should have known when it was time to stop. I wanted so badly to get back to skiing, back to my life, I could taste it. It had been my whole world; I lived to push down a hill at breakneck speed, nothing but wind and snow scraping under my skis. My body remembered it, my head remembered it more and I wanted it, I wanted it all back.

Everyone, the doctors, the trainers, Tin, looked at me sideways and wondered if I wasn't gone just a little crazy. I wasn't listening, not to them, not to my body, and in the process of not listening, I nearly lost all the mobility I'd fought so hard to regain in the weeks since my accident.

There was pain. Pain was nothing new. I pushed against it. And it wasn't any worse than it had ever been, an ache in my thigh, a complaint in my hip. Nothing a little Advil and a whirlpool wouldn't knock away.

I came back to Park City feeling good. It no longer hurt to walk around, and the pool workouts went well enough. I thought I could push harder. Hill training had always been a part of my regimen—I ran nearly every day, outside on the trails when I could manage it because the terrain was varied and the inclines challenging. So, the day after I came back from Tin's, I put on my running shoes and headed for the trails behind the condo.

It was full spring in the mountains now, the snow gone from the trails leaving traces of mud. The temperature rose, it would be near eighty degrees according to the local weather. I felt the breeze on my arms, the sun warming the back of my head and I was alive again. I concentrated on my steps and my breath until there was nothing but my pulse and the muscles of my legs, pushing me forward.

The pain crept in slowly, a small complaint like a creaky hinge in my hip. I ran through it, the endorphins had kicked in and I felt great. Another mile, and I turned down the trail that would wind back to the condo complex. The path was rock strewn and again I focused on my feet as I navigated the terrain. All the while, the pain blossomed, until it flowed through my legs and radiated up and down into my lower back. Still, I ignored it.

Another mile and I could see the trailhead and the parking lot of the complex beyond it. The pain was insistent now, stabbing at my hip with every step. I took a deep breath and pushed through it. Another hundred yards and my leg buckled under me, a pain so intense it made me fall to my knees, tears coming to my eyes unbidden.

I clenched my teeth and lay down on my back, the clear blue sky above the branches of newly leaved aspens. I ordered myself to get up, but my body was in no mood to listen to demands. I got onto my hands and knees, the best I could do, and crawled to the tree. I knelt there, with my forehead against the tree trunk, for what seemed like an eternity and waited for the pain to subside. It did, finally, and I used the trunk to pull myself to my feet and stood there another eternity, my arms around the tree.

The pain died down enough so that I could move forward, step, hop, step, stop, step, hop, pause, each step a new gamble; would the pain bring me down again? I moved that way until I got to the front door of my building.

I lived on the second floor and it took a long, long, time to negotiate the flight of stairs. Finally, though, I reached my refuge and I stood in my great room, the couch and throw the most welcome sight in the world. I wanted badly to sit down, but first I went to the medicine cabinet and found the prescription bottle for Percocet the doctor at the rehab had prescribed in case I needed it. "I guess I don't need to tell you to be careful with these?" he'd asked. I laughed at the thought, thinking I'd never take the damn things anyway. That was before now. I swallowed two down with water, then hobbled back to the living room and found my phone under the day's mail. I cursed myself for not taking the phone with me in the first place. I hobbled out to the porch and lowered myself into the wicker chair and called Dr. Reynolds at the orthopedic clinic in Salt Lake City. The Percocet had begun to work and I was starting to feel loopy. The pain was still there, but I didn't so much care about it.

The nurse listened as I told her who I was. "Of course we can make room for you, Ms. Whitmeyer. How about a week from next Thursday?"

The thought of being in this kind of pain for the next ten days nearly brought tears to my eyes again. "Do you have anything sooner?" I explained about jogging and the pain, leaving out the part about dropping to my knees and crawling around in the dirt.

"Can you hold?" I imagined her checking the schedule and hoped she'd be able to come with something.

"Mia?" The next voice was Dr. Reynolds. "What happened?"

I explained again. "I might have pushed too hard," I added and then nearly giggled in my Percocet-addled state at the understatement.

"On a scale of one to ten, how bad was the pain?"

I nearly said twelve but stopped myself. "Eight or nine."

He let out a long whistle. "And you got back to your condo?"

"I'm nothing if not determined." I smiled at my statement.

"How bad is it now?"

I assessed. I was feeling much better, the warm breeze coming in through the screened windows of my porch, the Percocet pushing the pain into a distance recess of my brain. "Three or four. I took pain meds."

"Okay, can you get yourself to the clinic tomorrow? I want to do an MRI on that hip as soon as possible."

I sat in the chair and watched the sun lower behind the butte. I was going to be fine. I'd pushed too hard, was all. The doorbell rang and I pulled myself up out of the chair and hobbled to the door. It hurt to walk, but not nearly as much as it had earlier, so I took this as a good sign. Creech stood on the threshold, with his hands in his pockets.

Part of me wanted to collapse into his arms, thankful he'd shown up when, maybe, I needed him and part of me wasn't willing to throw myself at anyone's feet, and particularly not at the man who haunted my dreams. "Can I come in?" he asked. I realized we were still at the door, me staring at him like he was an alien.

I stepped back. "Can I get you something? Tea, coffee?" God, I sounded like the hostess at the local diner. What the hell was wrong with me?

I must have been slurring my words, too, because he looked me over and asked. "Are you okay?"

"Sure, I'm dandy." I walked towards the kitchen.

"You're limping."

It was obvious, so I had to come clean. "Yes, I ran too hard today. I'm going to see Dr. Reynolds in the morning." The look in his eyes, so tender and concerned, was more than I could take, so I added, "I had this accident. You might have heard about it, it was all over the news. " His forehead creased, had I made him angry? "I was out on the porch, watching the sunset. It's probably done by now."

I hobbled back to the porch, mostly because I really, really needed to sit down, the ache in my hip had broken through the firewall set by the pain meds. I bit my lip as Creech settled into the other chair. "You're in pain." He took my hand.

I snatched it back. "Why are you here, anyway? Not to watch me wince. If you'd wanted to check on me you could have done that in e-mail. Or, hey, you could have called. Communication is easy in the digital age." I fisted my hand around the arm of the chair, I wanted to break something. I wanted the hurt gone.

Creech

I'd resigned and it had felt like a weight lifted from my shoulders. Only, that wasn't the hard part. The hard part was talking to Mia, letting her know, once and for all, everything in my heart. I'd arranged and rearranged the words in my head and then, when I got to her door, those words dropped away and I was left mute, with nothing but a whole bunch of feelings circling around in my head. It hadn't helped that she'd winced as she opened the door, then hobbled away from it. Her pain caught me completely unaware, though it shouldn't have after what she'd been through. Her anger caught me off guard, too. Though it shouldn't have, either.

I was pretty sure the anger was rooted in hurt. I had hurt her, I had stayed away and instead of it being a good thing, a noble thing, my absence had hurt her. The revelation hit me hard. "I'm sorry. You're right, I should have written. Or called."

"Or actually stopped by when you were going to"

I must have shown my surprise, because she added, "I talked to Katya. In fact, I've talked to just about everybody except for you."

What now? Would honesty work? It was the only thing I had. "I didn't want to get between you and Connor." I stood up. I couldn't look at her. Hell, I could barely get his name up out of my throat.

"Connor and I—"

I didn't want to hear it, so I held up my hand to stop her. Better say it now, it was now or never. "I can't let you go without telling you that I don't want you to be with Connor." I gathered up my strength and looked her in the eye. "If there's even a remote chance for us, I want to take it. To hell with timing, to hell with everything. I want you in my life, Mia. However I can get you, I want you." There was a break in my voice. I swallowed it down.

Mia blinked a few times and I realized she was crying. She stood up, hoisting herself out of the chair and hobbled the few steps between us. "I want you too," she whispered. Then she smiled. "Though I'm doped up on Percocet, so you might want to make your declaration later."

Mia

He laughed. "I'll make it a million times over." His hand was in my hair and then our lips met and there it was, that feeling, like flight, that happened every time he kissed me.

"It might be the drugs talking, but you are a damn fine kisser," I said into his ear. The dimple in his cheek came out when he smiled and I kissed it. Then the pain of standing up started to get to me and I lowered myself back into the wicker chair. His dimple faded. "I'm okay." I needed to reassure myself as well as him.

He sat back down in the other chair and took my hand and turned it over. "There's something else I ought to talk to you about. I quit."

"You what?"

"I handed in my resignation to Mike this morning."

I was too astonished to say anything. For a guy like Creech, an ex-racer, there was no better job than the one he'd aspired to for so many years. Another thought occurred to me, if he wasn't my coach anymore, there was nothing standing in our way. I'd never forgive myself if I was the reason for his quitting.

As though reading my thoughts, he said, "I didn't quit because of you, if that's what you're thinking. Not directly, anyway."

"What does that mean, not directly?" I thought about how hard I'd pushed him away. I didn't want to push him away anymore.

"Your accident did send me into a tailspin." He traced his finger up the line in my palm. The lifeline, it was called. "It was so much like my own—and the last thing I wanted was to relive my own accident. It was such a dark time for me. But then something happened, I started to examine my life, my priorities."

"And that led you to throw away the job you've spent the last ten years trying to get?"

"When you put it that way, it sounds crazy." He let out a laugh, then looked me in the eye again. "Have you ever wanted something so badly and then, when you got it, you realized you didn't want it after all? I'm not Marv, he gave his whole life over to racing—ruined two marriages doing it, from what I understand. I knew, somewhere along the line, I couldn't do it. I need more from my life."

I'd never given thought to Marv Eagan's personal life, but it was true. He'd given all his love to skiing and competition. Nell had been his third wife and his only son had barely spoken to him. I thought about my own attitude, how focused I'd been and how the focus had gone missing and, maybe for the first time, I could imagine this to be a good thing. Skiing had given me more than I could have hoped for, but it hadn't come cheap. I'd given it most of my adolescence and all of my adulthood so far. "What will you do?"

"I don't know. I've got some money saved, so for now I'll go up to Wilmington and fix my house. I've talked with Eric, I might go back into the family ski area business, help him run it. I'm thirty-one, and I figure it's a good time for me to change things, if I'm going to change them."

"I'll be thirty in August. Sometimes, it feels like I'm about a hundred." I squeezed his hand. "Connor and I split up. I broke it off." I took my other hand and ran it over his cheek. "I couldn't go back to him, because I'm in love with you." Those were about the truest words I'd ever spoken. I'd skied down steep mountains at breakneck speed and it had taken only half the courage it took to say them.

Creech pulled a strand of hair behind my ear. "Well, this is good. As it happens, I'm in love with you, too."

Twenty Two

Creech

Yes, I spent the night with her and no, I didn't make love to her. She was hopped up on pain meds and aching besides, which wasn't an ideal situation for romance. I couldn't and wouldn't have left her alone. She didn't ask me to stay, it happened. I think it was supposed to happen as it did. "I need a shower," she said. We'd been sitting on her porch, and what was left of the sun had faded under the butte and left us in the dark. "I'm afraid I'm going to kill myself by slipping in the damn tub."

I took her hand. In the bathroom, I helped her out of her clothes. The scar on her hip was puckered and angry, slicing through her skin. I traced my finger over it.

"Ouch, huh?" she said.

I got out of my own clothes and pointed to the zipper scar at my knee. "We match."

I turned on the water and we got under the warm spray. She braced her hands on my shoulders. "That feels so good," she said as she turned her face and let water cascade downward. I soaped the washcloth and ran it over her shoulders. I had an erection the size of Texas, but I wasn't going there. This was so much more than sex and we both knew it. I washed the scar on her hip and knelt to kiss it.

"You are so beautiful," I said.

"I am so banged up," she said.

"That's what makes you beautiful."

Afterwards, I toweled her dry and we lay naked in the sheets. She turned to put her head on my chest and

I stroked her hair, until we both fell asleep.

Her alarm went off at six and I woke, disoriented until I saw her head on the pillow next to mine and I knew exactly where I was and it was exactly where I was supposed to be. She opened her eyes, dreamy and tranquil.

And then she winced.

"You want pain meds?"

"No, I'll be okay." She tried to smile and leaned in to kiss me.

"What time's your appointment at the ortho clinic?"

"Ten."

"I'll drive you." I braced for an argument. Mia wasn't a woman who asked for or wanted help. I was ready to stand my ground and make her give in, this once.

"I'd like it if you did," she said.

Mia

Creech squeezed my hand as we rode the elevator to the radiation department on the third floor of the ortho clinic. I wanted to push the button to the ground floor, walk through the lobby and climb back into the cab of Creech's truck, but the pain in my hip insisted I follow through, put on my big girl panties, and face the exam. "I'm glad you're here," I told him as the doors slid open.

"Hell, I've got a couple of free hours."

The nurse who called my name at reception was pushing an empty wheelchair in front of her. "I don't need it," I said.

"You should sit," Creech said.

"I had enough of these things. I don't need it." I insisted. Then I took a few steps and decided maybe the nurse had it right after all. I sat down.

I'd had MRIs before, you don't get through years

of competition without a few bumps and bruises along the way, and then my accident had upped the need for diagnostics. For months, I'd spent my life at the mercy of these machines. The technician was polite and efficient and it was done quickly, though not quickly enough.

We went up to Dr. Reynold's office on the fourth floor and waited for the results in his waiting room. Reynolds himself came out to meet us a few minutes later. If he was surprised Creech was there with me, he didn't show it. He led us back to a conference room with projection screens on the wall.

Dr. Reynolds switched on one of the screens. The black and white of my hip looked like an abstract painting. There was an arrow pointing to a tiny black dot with a white halo around it. "That," said Dr. Reynolds, "is edema caused by stress. You have a few of them. The good news is the damage isn't permanent, with some rest you'll be back to normal."

Nothing serious. I felt a wave of relief until another thought left me cold. "And what's the bad news?"

"Well, Mia." Dr. Reynolds steepled his hands. "This is an indicator. You are at high risk of premature osteoarthritis. If you take care, you'll be fine. "

"Okay, so I'll lay off for a while. I can do that."

He raised his eyes and the look in them gave me more information than I needed. "It's more than that. The truth is, if you train at the level necessary for you to compete, you could do permanent damage."

"It could lead to osteoarthritis and cripple me?"

"Not could. Most likely will. I'm sorry, Mia."

The lump in my throat wouldn't let me answer him and the room began to swim away. I put my fingers to my eyes. I would not cry. Not here. Not now. Then Creech had his hand on my arm and then he was leading me back out to the elevators.

"I'm hungry and you haven't eaten." Creech pulled into the parking lot of a Chili's. We'd been driving for twenty minutes and those were the first words either of us had spoken.

I ordered food as though on autopilot. A salad of some kind, I couldn't have told you which.

"I'm here for you," Creech said once our food had come.

It wasn't as though I hadn't thought about the future. I'd spent the last few months imagining the end of my career, how I would feel when the end came. And now the end was here and I didn't feel much of anything at all. "I don't know if I can talk about it." Gratefully, he dropped the subject.

I asked him to stay the night. The idea of being alone in the dark was too much to bear. I kissed his neck, unbuttoned his shirt and he said, "Mia?" with a question mark in his voice.

"I'm fine. You're good at keeping me from thinking too hard."

He was tender, more tender than the last time, our first time together. Then, we'd come together like rockets in the dark, with a passion pent up for so long it was spectacular when we finally unleashed it. Now, after the accident, I had become less fiery. I was softer, more yielding. He whispered "I love you," as he came into me and the whole of it, the tenderness and all I'd gained and lost overcame me.

I couldn't hold back the tears afterward. I lay in his arms and let them roll down my cheeks and onto his chest. "I hope that's not a critique of my mad skills," he said, wiping my cheek with his finger.

Then I was laughing and crying. "No, not hardly." And we lay quiet in the dark.

Creech

She felt good in my arms, but it was hard, knowing how broken up she was. I lay there, unable to sleep, as she drifted off. Though she hadn't fallen asleep either. Her voice came up out of the darkness. "When did you know it was time to quit racing?"

I never talked to anyone about the time after my accident in Grindlewald, except to say it was a bad time and I'd moved past it. "I wasn't you." Even now, I wanted to tip toe around it.

"No. You were younger and you had your whole career in front of you."

"I wanted to come back. Hell, I would have sold my soul to the devil to come back. We were in summer camp, over at St. Mary's, and I skied a GS. It was never my best event, but God, I posted a time that wouldn't make the top thirty on the team let alone the top in the world. My knees felt like shit and the coach kept saying it would get better. I knew it wouldn't. There were thirty guys who could beat me standing near the finish line, I couldn't do it anymore." It hurt to bring it up even now.

"I'm going to Mike tomorrow. He'll want me to do a press conference. I'll have to tell my folks, the girls. I wish I could just slip away, unnoticed, but I can't. That's the hardest part, having to face them all, having to say it's over in public."

I pulled her tight. "I'll be right there with you. I won't let you go it alone."

Her lips brushed my shoulder then her cheek was on my chest again. "It's weird, I can't see past telling everyone. After is this big empty space and it scares the hell out of me. But then a part of me is ready to move on and it's exhilarating. I'm not making any sense."

"It makes all the sense in the world." I ran my fingers through her hair. "Come to Wilmington with me. We can take the truck, drive across the country. We can ride down Route 66. And then you can stay with me. The house is a big mess, but it's empty. We can go there together. Figure things out."

She raised her head off the pillow. "You mean it?"

"I've never been more serious about anything in my life. Come with me."

Mia

Retiring from ski racing was about the hardest thing I'd ever have to do. I don't know what I expected, lots of disappointment, I guess, and I didn't want to disappoint anyone. I was surprised how accepting the people I loved were. My dad told me I was doing the right thing and my mom said I should come to Franconia and bring Creech with me. Tin let out a war whoop and said it was perfect, me running off with the man I loved. Reni was happy I was in love and Rachel said I'd be a champion forever. And when I'd finished making my round of calls I realized they'd already come to terms with what I'd failed to see, the end had come when I was air evacuated off the mountain in Innsbruck. They were happy I was still breathing and maybe that was enough.

Mike took a few days to set up the press conference. I'd been in the spotlight and I needed to take my final bows, whether I wanted to or not. It was one thing to talk privately to the people who cared about me, it was another to put a public face on the end of my career. We chose the training center as the venue for my announcement. I thought it was the perfect place, but when I walked into the facility and saw the giant poster of me skiing for the gold in the downhill at the Vancouver Olympics, emotion hit me so hard I had to lean on Creech.

He squeezed my arm and, ever the coach, said, "You're bigger than this thing, Mia. Go get it." He sat in the front row next to me as Mike Granberg walked to the podium. He outlined my career, full of all these achievements and I was looking at it from far, far away, wondering if it was really me he was going on about.

Then it was my turn and I walked to the podium. I'd spent hours trying to figure out what to say. In the end, I went with a simple declaration about how much skiing had meant to me, how important it had been to my life, and how it was time for me to move on. The lump in my throat grew and my voice broke as I said the last. The room was so, so quiet, all of these reporters and photographers and people involved in ski racing looking at me. I stood there, breathing, trying hard to hold it together. Then, one by one, they stood up and began clapping, until the room was filled with their applause.

Twenty Three

Creech and I left for Wilmington the day after the press conference. It was hard to lock the door on my condo, it felt like the period at the end of one long stretch of my life. It also opened a new door, and as I stashed my suitcase behind the seat in the cab of Creech's truck, I felt the excitement of beginning.

All my life, I'd been focused on skiing, and I would forever love to ride the snow on skis, but that world had been small—my life built around competing and training. It had shrunk to the size of a hospital room after my accident and now, as we rode down the highway, the windows open, music on the radio, the world opened and there was so much of it, big and bright and waiting for us to find it.

We took the byways, secondary roads that wrapped themselves around mountains and followed rivers and intersected small towns. We stopped to admire the view. It took two weeks to get to Lake Placid. On the last day, I drove up Route 11, through the piney slopes of the Adirondacks. Creech, usually filled with commentary, got quiet, so quiet I asked if anything was wrong. "No. Just that we'll be there soon."

"We could drive back."

That got a smile, the small dimple in his mouth made my heart sing. "Can't go backwards, Mia."

We stopped for lunch in a deli in the small town of Tupper Lake, and then went to a farmer's market for apples and cheese and a bottle of wine for our arrival. Creech got behind the wheel and an hour later, we pulled into the driveway of an old brown shingled farmhouse with a porch running across the front of it.

"We've reached our destination," Creech said.

Creech had told me about his farmhouse, mostly describing it as decrepit, and I was expecting much worse. It was old, true enough. Several porch rails were missing and the floor boards were split in a few places. Maybe because it belonged to the man I loved, or maybe because it fit my view of home, I knew, the moment we pulled into the driveway, I would be happy here. "It's beautiful."

"Wait until you see the inside. I'll take the keys so you can't run off with the truck."

We stepped around a ladder in a foyer where the floor was covered in a tarp. The molding over the door to the living room had been newly painted, the wood on the stairs was worn and in need of refinishing. There were several cabinet doors leaning against the walls in the kitchen, the cabinets they belonged on open, the shelves empty. More than half of the doors had been beautifully restored, dark pine varnished to a mirror shine. "You have a hidden talent for renovation," I said as he led the way upstairs to a bedroom void of anything but a sleeping bag stashed in the corner.

"It's got good bones, or so the realtor who talked me into buying said." Creech tapped a foot against the floor board. "These are wide plank floors, you'd pay a fortune for new ones. I'm going to refinish them. And paint. And—it's a very long list."

I smirked at him. "If I were into conspiracy theories, I'd think you invited me here so you could cop some free labor."

"You got me." He gazed at me with a dazed kind of smile and took a deep breath. "I hope it will be our house."

"You want to sell me half?"

"You aren't making this easy." He took me by the hand and led me back down to the stairs to the front porch. "I've got three acres, all woods."

I looked out to see the birches nestled around the house, the afternoon light playing through them. "Honestly, you don't need to sell me."

"Good God, I am making a mess of this. Chalk it up to being nervous. I've been trying to figure out how to do this since we left Park City. I thought we'd stop at a park, or maybe have dinner in a fancy restaurant. And then it came to me I had to do it here. Right here, on the front porch of the farmhouse. It was tough waiting. Today was murder, I thought we'd never get here." He fished through his pocket and then dropped to one knee holding out a ring. "Marry me, Mia."

A million thoughts raced through my head. They were all muted by one big shout coming up from my heart. A resounding yes. Yes, this was exactly what I wanted, this house, this man, this life with him. I was astoundingly sure, as sure as I was of my own name. I got down on my knees, tears in my eyes. "I love you."

"Please say that means yes."

"Yes." I kissed him and then whispered. "Yes, yes, yes," into his ear.

Epilogue

Mia

I've gathered up new memories now, memories that have nothing to do with winning or losing or falling. Unless, of course, you consider falling in love. I was head-over-heels for Creech Creches and each day we spend together, the life we were building made that love deeper and stronger.

Winning a gold cup will always be a cherished memory. But winning Creech? That one is just as good. We're married now, and our wedding day was nearly perfect.

Neither of us wanted to wait, so in September, having given my mom just enough time to plan all the details, we got married in the garden at my parents' inn. The day started out as cloudy, I remember a few raindrops on the windowpane in my childhood bedroom where I'd been too excited to sleep well. More excited, in fact, than I recall being before a race. The rain caused some worry, but by mid-morning, a southwest breeze had chased the grey clouds away, leaving the sun to peek out behind puffy cumulous. The temperatures rose into the seventies, making it a picture perfect day for a garden wedding. I remember taking the vintage ivory colored gown Mom and I had purchased the week before out of the garment bag. It hung over the door as Mom and Tin fussed over my hair. The sapphire necklace that had belonged to my grandmother, which Mom hung proudly around my neck, telling me it covered three of the basic four—borrowed, blue, and old. I remember looking in the mirror once zipped into the dress, the photographer snapping a few photos.

Tin, my best lady in all things, was dressed in a blue silk gown. She'd picked it out herself and thanked me again for not making her wear something hideous.

"I'm nervous," I admitted to Tin as I peered out at all the guests seated in the garden.

Then Creech stood at the gazebo set up for the occasion, looking good in a suit. And Tin said, "You just march up there, take that man by the hand, and you've got this."

"Eyes on the prize," I said, using the phrase we'd often used in our racing days.

"Eyes on the prize," Tin repeated.

Then my dad, tears in his eyes, offered me his arm. The quartet in the garden began to play. And as I walked down the aisle, everything and everyone dropped away except for Creech. His eyes, green as the hemlocks growing on the hills, were filled with all the love I felt.

"Let's do this thing," he whispered to me when I'd taken his hand.

"Yes," I said, "let's."

And we turned to the minister and we did.

About Ute

Ute (who pronounces her name Oooh-tah) Carbone is an award winning author of women's fiction, comedy, and romance. She and her husband live in New Hampshire, where she spends her days walking, eating chocolate and dreaming up stories.

www.ingramcontent.com/pod-product-compliance
Lightning Source LLC
Chambersburg PA
CBHW011842220626
47052CB00008B/1255